BOOKS BY MARY TOWNE
FIRST SERVE
GOLDENROD

GOLDENROD

GOLDENROD

by Mary Towne

NEW YORK *Atheneum* 1977

Library of Congress Cataloging in Publication Data
Towne, Mary.
      Goldenrod.
      SUMMARY: Goldenrod is an unusual babysitter who
uses her special means of travel to entertain her charges.
      [1. Baby sitters—Fiction] I. Title.
PZ7.T6495Go   [Fic]   77-1578
ISBN 0-689-30597-4

For my three stay-at-homes

Contents

CHAPTER 1	LOOKING FOR A BABY-SITTER	*3*
CHAPTER 2	GOLDENROD	*10*
CHAPTER 3	GOLDENROD'S TRIP	*21*
CHAPTER 4	SOME EXPLANATIONS	*33*
CHAPTER 5	VAL'S TRIP	*44*
CHAPTER 6	SOME DECISIONS	*57*
CHAPTER 7	LAUREL'S TRIP	*69*
CHAPTER 8	GOLDENROD AT WORK	*85*
CHAPTER 9	SUSAN'S TRIP	*95*
CHAPTER 10	HEATH'S TRIP	*113*
CHAPTER 11	DAISY'S TRIP	*130*
CHAPTER 12	GOLDENROD'S STORY	*146*
CHAPTER 13	MRS. MADDER'S TRIP	*158*
CHAPTER 14	PEARLY	*174*

GOLDENROD

Chapter 1 _Looking for a Baby-Sitter_

Mrs. Rose Madder had five children and a housekeeper named Miss Vetch.

She needed the housekeeper because of her job in the city, working for a magazine. Mrs. Madder was an artist who would really have preferred to stay at home painting pictures; but ever since Mr. Madder had left them to go off and make sculptures (he was an artist, too) , Mrs. Madder had worked to support her family.

She liked her job well enough. After all, she was in charge of how the magazine looked, which was a big responsibility. Mrs. Madder was the person who made sure the illustrations got onto the right pages and saw that all the margins came out even. But it must be confessed that all the time she was doing her job, Mrs. Madder was secretly painting pictures in her head. In her

spare time at home, she turned these into real pictures
—so many of them that every wall in the house was covered with her paintings. There was even a painting in
the garage.

As for Miss Vetch . . . well, since she will be leaving this story almost immediately, there are only a few
things you need to know about her. She was a good cook
and kept the house very clean. She washed the kitchen
floor three times a week and always remembered to write
down telephone messages. Mrs. Madder told people she
never had to worry about a thing, with Miss Vetch in the
house—except, perhaps about why none of them had
ever really liked Miss Vetch.

"She's always smiling," Susan Madder said.

"But only with her face," said Val, the oldest boy. He
tried to explain what he meant. "She's all sweet and nice
on the outside, but inside—well, inside she's *sour.*"

"Like those pears you buy in the middle of winter,"
Mrs. Madder agreed, in spite of herself. "So yellow and
ripe-looking—but then, when you bite into them—"

"They're hard," said Daisy, the youngest, making a
face.

"And bitter," said Heath.

Heath had the most cause to dislike Miss Vetch, because Heath was a wanderer. Or so Miss Vetch said.
Heath thought of himself as a traveler—or better yet, an
explorer. He liked to be out and about, roaming around,
keeping on the move. But although he never got into
trouble and was always home in time for supper, Miss
Vetch disapproved. "Where have you been?" she would
demand, forgetting to smile. It wasn't really a question.
What she meant was, wherever you've been, you

4

shouldn't have gone there. Miss Vetch believed in people staying put.

"Anyway," said Laurel, the eldest of Mrs. Madder's children, "we don't need her any more."

"We don't?" Mrs. Madder was surprised. But she looked at Laurel with respect. Laurel's ideas usually made sense.

"Well we're all in school now," Laurel pointed out. "And with five of us, we could take care of the house ourselves. If everybody had chores to do—"

"I could make a chart!" Susan interrupted, her black eyes snapping. Susan loved things like making charts— drawing straight lines with a ruler and writing labels in small neat letters. Also Susan was bossy and liked to keep track of what everyone else was doing.

"What about cooking?" Val asked. "I mean—well, like supper." Val led an active life, what with friends and sports and special projects, and always had an appetite.

"Oh, I could manage the cooking," Mrs. Madder replied, rather absently. She was thinking what a joy it would be not to come home to Miss Vetch's cheery smile, especially when she was feeling tired. "I like to cook, or at least I used to. Of course we might not eat until rather late. . . . No, the real problem would be the afternoons, after school."

"Oh, Mother!" the children protested. "We can take care of ourselves, we're old enough now—"

"No," said Mrs. Madder, who could be quite firm when she wanted to be. "Someone has to be in charge, and Laurel's not old enough. Or even if she is, it wouldn't be fair to her."

Mrs. Madder had strong feelings about eldest children, having been one herself. It was so easy to wind up acting like a policeman and having everyone else hate you.

"And anyway we need someone who can drive. In case of emergencies and birthday parties and things like that," she explained.

"We could get a baby-sitter," Daisy said hopefully. All her friends had baby-sitters; but because Miss Vetch had been with them ever since Daisy was born, she hardly ever got to have a sitter, except sometimes on weekends.

"Yes, I suppose we could," Mrs. Madder said slowly. The others looked at Daisy with approval. "A high school girl, maybe—someone reliable—"

"Someone who'd *do* things with us," Susan said. "Like playing Parcheesi when it rains—"

"Or Chinese checkers," said Heath. Actually he thought it was a boring kind of game; but he liked the idea of China.

"Well, yes," said their mother. "But reliability is the main thing." She sighed. "Maybe a girl isn't such a good idea, after all. An older woman—"

"No, somebody young! Please, Mother," the children pleaded. "And the *really* main thing is to have someone we like."

"Well . . ." Mrs. Madder looked at them and smiled. "All right. I'll see what I can do."

So Miss Vetch departed, with her ruffled aprons and her African violet plant and her smile; and the children took over the house.

Susan drew up a chart and pinned it to the kitchen bulletin board. For the first few days, she marched importantly around the house making sure that everybody was doing what they were supposed to do. But they were all so glad to be rid of Miss Vetch that they worked with a will. Soon the chores became routine. And now there was nobody to throw away Daisy's collection of horse chestnuts or to disturb Val's miniature water wheel experiment in the basement washtub.

Maybe the house wasn't quite as tidy as it had been before—but at least, as they all agreed, you could *find* things.

The only thing they couldn't find was the right baby-sitter.

Heaven knows they tried. The children called up friends who had older sisters. Mrs. Madder got lists of baby-sitters from her friends and put up a notice at the local high school. "After all," she said, "we can't just hire *anybody*. We have to know something about the person first."

The sitters came and went. Sometimes, after the first few days, they didn't come at all. There was a football game after school or a sick friend they had to visit or they'd changed their minds about the job. There were too many kids to keep track of, they complained; it was hard enough just remembering their names.

Sometimes the sitters came late (the car wouldn't start) . Sometimes they left early (they had to wash their hair or go downtown before the stores closed) . Of those who stayed, one just sat and watched TV. Another spent all her time on the telephone. A third did her homework, with the record player turned up so high the neighbors complained.

The only sitter the children really liked was a very tall skinny boy named Malcolm, who learned all their names right away and who taught them to play poker.

But then the coach of the high school track team persuaded Malcolm to become a hurdler. Malcolm had a natural talent for jumping over things, it seemed; he might even be Olympic material. The children hoped for Malcolm's sake that the coach was right and resigned themselves to yet another sitter.

This one was the niece of an acquaintance of Mrs. Madder's, said to be sweet, dependable, and very fond of animals. Since the Madders had no pets, Mrs. Madder couldn't imagine what this had to do with anything; but she soon found out.

The animal the sitter was fond of turned out to be her own dog, Whiffles, who came with her every day and who occupied most of her attention. Whiffles was a tiny creature with hardly any hair. He caught cold easily, the sitter explained, and needed to have the heat turned on every day, no matter what the weather was outside. Mrs. Madder would come home from work on a sunny fall day to find the thermostat at eighty degrees and Whiffles lying on the couch wrapped up in her best blue blanket.

"I can't afford the fuel bills," she said in despair one evening. Looking at the flushed faces of her children, she added, "And you're the ones who're going to catch cold at this rate, and I can't afford the doctor bills, either. . . . Oh dear. Maybe we'd better try and get Miss Vetch back."

There was a chorus of protest. The children said that even Whiffles was better than Miss Vetch.

"Why don't we try putting an ad in the paper?" Laurel suggested.

Mrs. Madder looked doubtful. "But anyone can answer an ad."

"That's why," Heath said. "I mean, we knew about all

8

these other sitters, and they weren't any good. Maybe we need someone who just *happens*."

"Like a grab bag," Daisy agreed.

"Well. . . ."

Mrs. Madder rubbed her forehead tiredly. Aside from anything else, this baby-sitter problem was beginning to interfere with her painting. She no longer saw so many fascinating pictures in her mind, just waiting to be painted. Sometimes, on weekends when she went up to her studio in the attic, all she saw on the blank canvas before her was a sulky-looking teenager carrying a pile of schoolbooks—or worse yet, Whiffles wrapped up in the blue blanket.

"Maybe you're right," she told the children. "It's worth a try, anyway."

So they made up an ad to go in the local paper under HELP WANTED. The ad said:

> Reliable baby-sitter needed for school-age children. Weekday afternoons, 3–6 P.M. Must have own car and like to play games. Reasonable pay, no animals.

"Whose animals, theirs or ours?" Val objected. "That sounds confusing."

"Just no animals on either side," his mother said. "It seems perfectly clear to me."

"Shouldn't we say how *many* children?" Susan asked.

"Oh, a good baby-sitter won't mind how many," Mrs. Madder said confidently. "The more the merrier." She sealed the envelope, stamped it, and sent it off to the newspaper.

And that was how Goldenrod came into their lives.

Chapter **2** *Goldenrod*

"Is that really your name?" Susan asked. *"Golden-rod?"*

The new sitter hung up her jacket neatly in the hall closet and turned to the children.

"Why not?" she said, with a shrug. "I think it's kind of a pretty name, myself."

At first glance she didn't look much older than Laurel —a thin girl in jeans and a faded plaid shirt, with a mass of springy golden hair and large green eyes in a pale, heart-shaped face.

"But goldenrod"—

"Gives you hay fever," finished Heath. He pretended to sneeze, and Daisy giggled. Laurel frowned at them.

"That's ragweed, not goldenrod," said the new sitter. "It comes out at the same time. I thought everybody knew *that*."

But Goldenrod didn't sound offended. She went into the living room and then stopped dead.

"Wow!" she said. "You sure have a lot of pictures."

She walked over to the fireplace and stood staring at the big painting above the mantel. It was a black square across which long fine strands of color were drifting as if blown by a wind—pale green, yellow, silver.

"Our mother's an artist," Heath explained. "That's a willow tree."

Goldenrod studied the painting for another moment, and then shook her head decisively. "I like it all right," she said. "But that's no willow tree, not by me."

She moved on to inspect another painting—faces this time, but so blurred by the rain (or snow?) that seemed to be falling in the picture, you could hardly make them out. Over her shoulder she asked, "What does your dad do?"

There was a little silence. Then Laurel said "He's an artist, too. But he doesn't live with us any more."

"Divorced, huh?"

The children looked at one another. Divorced? They didn't really know. "Going our own ways," was how their mother had put it, seeming quite cheerful about it at the time. They shrugged—all except Daisy, whose eyes filled with tears, as they always did at the mention of the father she had never seen.

"He sends us presents at Christmas," Susan volunteered. "Except when he forgets. But Mother says it's Christmas he forgets, not us."

"Absent-minded." Goldenrod nodded. "Some people are like that. Not so easy to live with, I guess." She glanced at the children. "Hey—I hope you didn't mind my asking. About your dad, I mean."

They shook their heads. Goldenrod was wandering on into the kitchen. "More pictures!" she exclaimed, looking at the watercolors pinned to the cabinet doors. Then she said abruptly, "You kids got some peanut butter around, by any chance?"

"We're not supposed to eat between meals," Daisy said primly.

"That's you, not me. I just came from my job at the supermarket," Goldenrod explained, "and I never did get to have lunch. One of the other girls was out sick, so I had to work straight through." She opened a cupboard door.

"A supermarket?" Susan was bewildered. "But there's all that food there!"

"Not sandwiches," Goldenrod pointed out. "Not unless you make them yourself. Can you see me making myself a peanut butter sandwich right there at the checkout counter? In front of all the customers?"

Daisy giggled, and even Val smiled. He had kept a scowling silence up to now. He was getting sick and tired of this whole baby-sitter business—having to hang around and be polite to each new arrival. Besides, there was a baseball game going on in the vacant lot down the street.

"Is that what you do?" Laurel asked. "Work at the checkout counter?"

Goldenrod nodded. "Add 'em up, ring 'em up, check 'em out. I'm fast, too—good hands."

They all looked at her hands, deftly spreading peanut butter on a slice of bread.

Val gave a snort. "Good hands—that sounds like a ballplayer."

"You ought to see me pitch sometime," Goldenrod told him seriously. "Girls' softball league, back in Ohio. Nineteen and three one year, including a no-hitter." She took a bite of her sandwich.

Daisy opened her mouth to ask what nineteen and three meant, but Heath said, "Is that where you're from? Ohio?"

"For a while," Goldenrod said vaguely. "I move around a lot. Just trying places out—you know."

Heath did know; but he couldn't help wondering about things like school and parents and money (for bus fare). How old was Goldenrod, anyway? Laurel was wondering the same thing. Goldenrod wore eye makeup and big gold hoop earrings—but so did a lot of the older kids at school. Eighteen, maybe? Twenty?

Susan was still thinking about the supermarket. She said, "But if you already have a job, Goldenrod, why do you want this one, too?"

"I can use the money," Goldenrod said. "Besides—" She shrugged. "I have my afternoons free, so why not? I like to keep busy."

They could all think of much better things to do with a free afternoon than working; but they didn't say so. Maybe, if Goldenrod was new in town, she was feeling a little lonely. Well, life in the Madder household would soon take care of that!

Goldenrod finished her sandwich and poured herself a glass of milk. "So," she said, regarding the five children over the rim of the glass with her sea-green eyes. "What's the deal?"

13

They looked blank.

"Well, I only talked to your Mom over the phone. She said be here at three and leave at six, when she gets home from work. So what else? I play games with you, like the ad said? Or I do laundry, sweep floors, cook— like that? I don't care either way," she explained earnestly. "I just need to know. I mean, if I take a job, I try to do it right."

Laurel explained about the chores. "Val has the vacuuming and the kitchen floor. I do laundry and ironing and making beds. Heath has washing the dishes and taking out the trash, and Susan cleans the bathrooms. And Daisy—"

"I dust," Daisy said proudly. "I'm a very good duster, Mother says so. Except I can't reach the tops of the pictures yet. I'm only six," she added, in the baby voice they all detested.

"Hey!" Goldenrod looked at them with respect. "That's pretty good—a bunch of kids like you. And the house looks good, too. Nice and clean." She rinsed out her glass at the sink and went back into the living room, the children trailing after her.

"You never know what you're getting into, answering an ad," she remarked, pausing to squint at another of Mrs. Madder's pictures—a very small painting of what seemed to be an apple, except that it was bright blue and had an orange stem. "Not just the job, I mean. The people, too."

Val thought of pointing out that they didn't know anything about Goldenrod either, as far as that went. But then, that was the whole idea, he remembered confusedly.

"Like . . . well, for instance"—Goldenrod thought a

14

moment—"you kids could be a bunch of cat burglars, for all I know."

"We *could?*" said Heath.

"Sure. Some of the big mobs, I read where they use kids all the time. Little enough to get through a basement window, or—"

"Or slide down the chimney," Daisy said excitedly. Laurel had been reading *Water Babies* to her.

"Or pick pockets," Val said, in spite of himself. He'd watched the movie of *Oliver Twist* on TV a few nights before.

"Yeah, stuff like that."

But Goldenrod settled herself comfortably on the old green couch, seemingly unconcerned at the prospect of baby-sitting for a den of thieves. She said, "Okay. Now the first thing is to get everybody's names straight. Let's go around the room once, starting with the oldest, and then I'll close my eyes and see if I've got you memorized."

They sat down obediently around the living room, though Val cast a yearning glance at the bright October afternoon beyond the windows. When they'd all said their names in turn, Goldenrod leaned back and shut her eyes.

"Okay. First there's Laurel. Long reddish hair and brown eyes. Kind of serious and worried-looking. And she's about—fourteen?"

"Thirteen," said Laurel, who was tall for her age. She didn't mind about the extra year; but her hair wasn't red, it was auburn—her mother said so. And as for looking worried . . . well, that was only because of trying to find the right baby-sitter. This struck her funny, and she smiled to herself.

15

"Then there's your brother," Goldenrod went on, "the one with the dark hair and eyes who doesn't say very much—that's Val. He looks about twelve, and I bet he's good at sports. Probably he's good at anything he really wants to do." She paused, but kept her eyes shut. "What's Val short for?"

"Valerian," said Daisy, before anyone could stop her.

They held their breaths. Val hated his name, and hardly anyone outside the family knew what it was. Once a boy at school had teased him by calling him Prince Valiant, and Val had knocked him down. But there *was* a princely kind of look about Val, they thought secretly. He was strong and broad-shouldered and always held himself very straight without even having to think about it.

But Val only scowled fiercely at Daisy and said nothing. Maybe he was mollified by Goldrenrod's remark about sports and being good at things. Or maybe he felt that since Goldenrod had an odd kind of name herself, she was in no position to laugh at his.

Goldenrod went on to Heath. "Straight blond hair," she said, "and those crazy blue eyes."

Now it was Heath's turn to squirm. He had wide-set eyes of an unusually clear, soft shade of blue.

"He has a kind of dreamy look too, like he's miles away some of the time. But he has a great smile." Goldenrod smiled a little to herself as she said this. It was true that people always seemed to smile back at Heath; and when he laughed, no one could resist him.

"Now let's see. . . ." Goldenrod pondered. "Heath must be about ten, so that makes Susan nine."

Susan sat up straighter in her chair. In spite of herself, she was impressed—indeed, they all were. Unless

Goldenrod was peeking? They stared at her suspiciously; but her eyes seemed firmly closed.

"Susan looks a little like Val," Goldenrod continued. "Except her face is rounder and her cheeks are redder. She has a kind of determined look. Also she's very neat and tidy."

No one contradicted this. Susan was nothing if not determined. And zippers never broke for Susan; buttons stayed on. Even her socks seemed to stay cleaner than anyone else's.

"So that just leaves Daisy. Curly blond hair and dimples and long eyelashes. . . . But I bet she's tougher than she looks. She'd have to be, just to keep up with the rest of you."

This was an aspect of Daisy the others had never considered. They were thinking about it when Goldenrod opened those strange green eyes of hers wide and said, "Well? Did I do okay?"

They nodded. Even Val had to admit to himself, grudgingly, that Goldenrod was even quicker than Malcolm had been. And she'd not only learned their names, she'd learned their faces, too.

Goldenrod said, "What does your mother look like? Is she pretty?"

Pretty? They'd never really thought about it.

"Well—not exactly," Laurel said. "She's tall and thin—"

"And she moves around fast," Daisy said. "Except when she's thinking about something."

"She has blue eyes like Heath's," Susan put in, "and dark hair. Only it's getting kind of gray now. She says every time we have a fight she gets another gray hair."

"Well, you'd better not have any fights while I'm

17

around," Goldenrod told them. "That's one thing I can't stand."

Heath said, "Oh, we don't really fight. We just argue sometimes." He gave her his disarming smile.

"Didn't you use to fight with your brothers and sisters?" Daisy asked curiously.

But Goldenrod didn't seem to have heard. She gave a sudden yawn and said, "Well. . . . What do you kids want to do today?"

They stirred uneasily in their chairs. They were all dying to get outside, except Laurel, who had homework to do. But they felt it might be rude to go off and leave Goldenrod alone on her very first day. Val thought of asking if she wanted to play ball; he was determined to check out that no-hitter story at the first opportunity. But maybe she was tired from her job, standing on her feet at the checkout counter all day.

Goldenrod seemed to have forgotten her own question. She was rummaging around for something in the depths of a large, battered-looking shoulder bag.

"Do you live near here?" Susan asked politely, to break the silence. "You and your family, I mean?"

Goldenrod looked up. Her green eyes had gone strangely cloudy and blank, as if a shadow had passed over them. "No," she said after a moment. "I live alone."

"Well, do you have your own apartment, then?" Susan persisted. "Or—" She stopped as Laurel shook her head at her. Being polite is one thing, Laurel's look said; being nosy is another.

Goldenrod seemed to have found what she was looking for—a crumpled envelope. She stared at it for a moment, sighed, and stuffed it back into her bag. Then she tipped her head back against the couch and folded her arms, looking thoughtful.

The children studied the new sitter, trying to make up their minds about her. She was *different*, anyway, they decided. No stupid questions about school or what they wanted to be when they grew up. No TV, no telephoning, no homework. And she'd only had a peanut butter sandwich and a glass of milk—not like another sitter they'd had, who'd eaten up half a chocolate cake in the course of an afternoon.

Also, she didn't do a lot of smiling. Which was fine with the Madder children, after so many years of being smiled at relentlessly by Miss Vetch . . . except that there was something about Goldenrod that made you *want* to see her smile, or even laugh once in a while. Maybe she just didn't have much sense of humor. Anyway, they decided, they liked her sensible, no-nonsense manner. Things wouldn't be complicated with Goldenrod around—that was what they felt.

On the other hand, if she was just going to *sit* all the time. . . .

Goldenrod yawned again. Was she falling asleep? Her eyes were almost closed.

In the unaccustomed silence (it was hardly ever silent in the Madder household), the children themselves began to feel drowsy. And now there was the oddest sensation of floating—of drifting and sliding—of slipping away. . . .

Like going down a water slide, Laurel thought dreamily. That smooth, slippery feeling, gliding swiftly down and down; and then the delicious splash, the cool water closing around you. . . .

19

Except that there wasn't any splash. Nor, when they managed to open their eyes at last, was there anything cool about the place in which they found themselves.

For the familiar room had disappeared, and so had the crisp October day. They were standing instead on the glaring, sun-baked pavement of a strange hot town called Gorseville—a town none of them had ever heard of before.

Chapter 3 Goldenrod's Trip

They knew the place was called Gorseville because of the signs. Gorseville Grain & Seed, Gorseville Electric, Gorseville Center Café. . . . If this was the center of it, Gorseville couldn't be a very big town, Val decided groggily, blinking into the strong sunlight. There were only a few blocks of stores, and where the sidewalks ended, the road had a dusty, country look to it.

"You kids wait here a minute," Goldenrod's voice said briskly. "I have to ask directions. I'll be right back."

The screen door of the hardware store slapped shut behind her. An old dog sleeping just outside stirred and twitched in a dream. Automatically the children moved back into the shade of a striped awning.

"Oh, it's so *hot!*" Daisy rubbed her eyes. "Why is it so hot here?"

"Take off your sweater," Susan said practically. But her own wool knee socks were already itching uncomfortably, and her school dress felt like a suit of armor.

"Do you think we could all be having the same dream?" Laurel asked the question curiously, but without any particular feeling of alarm.

A boy rode by on a bike, barefoot and eating a melting popsicle. He looked real enough, they all thought enviously.

"Maybe it's Goldenrod's dream," Susan suggested, "and we just happened to come along inside it."

Which, as it turned out, wasn't far from the truth.

And of course you don't argue with a dream, you just have it. Still (as they all agreed afterwards) it was certainly very odd, the way they simply accepted the situation—calmly and without fuss. Even Val, who normally hated being dragged places against his will, looked only mildly annoyed.

Mainly what they all felt was *hot*.

Daisy said hopefully, "Maybe we'll get to go swimming while we're here."

"In October?" Laurel said.

"Well, it feels more like August," Susan pointed out. "Maybe it's still summer here."

"Hey—pumpkins!" Heath was pointing at the market across the street. "So it must be October, if Hallowe'en's coming here, too."

"Well, I certainly hope we'll be home before *then!*" Laurel had just remembered the chapter she was supposed to read for social studies tomorrow. And there was math, too, and French verbs . . .

"I think we're down South somewhere," Heath said thoughtfully. "We'd have to be, for it to be this hot in

October. And anyway, the trees are different, sort of, and the smells." But he couldn't explain just what he meant.

Goldenrod came out of the hardware store then, followed by a fat man in overalls. The old dog woke up and growled, and the man said, "You, Fleabane—you git!" The dog slunk off down the street.

The fat man turned to Goldenrod. "Now, you just bear left at the fork, little lady, and then you watch out for the old creek road, on past Miss Hepatica's place. It's just up that way a piece—yellow house, with a big old pecan tree in the yard. But I don't know. . . ." He scratched his head. "Too bad they ain't on the telephone. It does seem to me I heard they'd moved out. Last week it was, or mebbe the week before."

Goldenrod looked dismayed. "But my letter—" She held up the crumpled envelope and squinted her green eyes at it, trying to make out the postmark.

"Mails are slow these days," the fat man said with a shrug. "And old Verne, over to the post office, he was laid up with the rheumatism awhile back—likely that held things up some."

"Well. . . ." Goldenrod hesitated. "Is it very far? Out to the house, I mean?" She pointed to the children and explained, "It's a baby-sitting job. I have to get them home by six."

Laurel was relieved; she'd be able to get her homework done after all, after supper. Heath nudged Susan and whispered, "See? He's got a Southern accent."

"Oh, it's no more'n a couple of miles." But the fat man looked doubtfully at their clothes. "You all ain't exactly dressed for walking, though."

"I know," Goldenrod said vaguely. "If I'd known we

were coming today—but I didn't. I mean, it just sort of happened."

What just sort of happened?

But nobody asked. Instead Daisy said timidly as they started off, "Who are we looking for, Goldenrod?"

"My friend Pearly," Goldenrod sounded surprised, as if they should have known. "Pearly Everlasting. I've been meaning to come visit her ever since she moved down here to Gorseville." She shook her yellow head. "It just shows you shouldn't put things off. I mean, unless I'm lucky and she's gone someplace like—oh, Georgia, or Grand Rapids—"

She broke off in the middle of this puzzling speech to say contritely, "Hey, I hope you all don't *mind* about this. I just thought, as long as we're here, anyhow. . . . But it might be kind of a long walk out to Pearly's house. We can go home right now, if you'd rather."

But she looked so disappointed at the thought that they assured her they didn't mind walking. This way they'd get to see something of the countryside, Heath said, explaining that they'd never been down South before.

Had Goldenrod? they wondered. Her own voice seemed to have taken on a slight Southern tinge in the last few minutes. Maybe the South was one of the places she'd tried out.

At first their way led past houses with big shade trees in the yards, and flowering shrubs and vines and small bright gardens. The air was heavy with the rich, sweet smell of magnolias. Funny how everything seemed to be in bloom at once, Laurel thought.

Then the paved road gave way to dirt, and they

emerged into the full glare of the afternoon sun. Culti-
vated fields stretched away on either side, bearing a bewildering variety of crops. Tobacco, cotton, peanuts,
corn; watermelons and sweet potatoes and beans and
spinach. . . . When they came to what looked like a
field of sugar cane, Laurel opened her mouth to say
something—but it was really too much effort to talk in
this heat. The road had begun to seem endless, with the
sun beating down on their bare heads and the dust rising
about their ankles as they walked.

After they reached the fork, the going was easier—
downhill, and shaded by occasional trees. They passed a
weatherbeaten cabin—Miss Hepatica's place?—and came
at last to the creek road. This was little more than a track
that wound its way through lush green undergrowth
into deeper woods. They couldn't see the creek, but
they could hear it bubbling and chuckling away somewhere off to their left.

"Mosquitoes," Val grumbled, slapping at one.

"Well, at least it's a little cooler here," Susan said
breathlessly.

Her face was fiery red, and her dress was sticking to
her shoulder blades. Indeed, they were all sweaty and
tired and irritable now, though no one had actually
complained—not even Daisy, who was getting a blister
on one heel from her new school shoes.

"It can't be much farther now," Goldenrod said over
her shoulder. "Oh, I hope Pearly's still here!"

But when they turned up the narrow dirt driveway
and found the yellow house standing in its clearing, just
as the fat man had said, they knew at once that the place
was deserted. A tire swing hung motionless from the big

pecan tree in the yard, and weeds were already choking the flower bed by the front porch. A doll with one arm missing lay forlornly in the thick grass beside the driveway.

Goldenrod picked up the doll and stood staring up at the house for a moment. She started to drop the doll into her big shoulder bag, but then seemed to check herself. Instead she replaced it gently on the grass and turned to the children.

"Well, that's that," she said with a shrug. "All that long walk for nothing. You poor kids. Some baby-sitter I turned out to be!"

She spoke lightly, but they could see how bad she felt about missing her friend Pearly. They were standing about awkwardly in the hot silence, trying to think of something cheerful to say, when a voice behind them demanded angrily:

"What you want here? You, girl—what you doin', hangin' around this house?"

They spun around, to see a tiny, grim-faced black woman standing at the bottom of the driveway. She was pointing a shotgun at them.

For a moment they were all speechless.

Then Goldenrod said in a scared voice, "Hey! Put that thing down, will you? I mean, I'm responsible for these kids, and— Please, ma'am, I was just looking for Pearly! She's a friend of mine."

"Pearly's gone." But the old woman seemed to relax a little; at least she lowered the shotgun.

"I know. I mean, I didn't know until I got here—"

"Moved away last week," said the old woman, nodding to herself. "Her daddy got himself a new job up North somewhere. I'm watching the house for them, time they send for the rest of their things." She paused, still eyeing Goldenrod suspiciously. "You a friend of Pearly's, you say?"

Goldenrod nodded. "I've got a letter from her right here." She began to fumble for it in her bag.

"Your name be Goldenrod, by any chance?"

When Goldenrod nodded again, the old woman's face broke into a smile, and she came forward slowly to shake hands. They saw she must be very old indeed, the way her face wrinkled up when she smiled, like a charred piece of paper.

"Well, now! This is purely a pleasure. I'm Miss Hepatica. Pearly was always talkin' about her friend Goldenrod. She'll be real sorry when she finds out she missed you."

Miss Hepatica looked at the children, and her old eyes twinkled. "Gave you younguns a scare, did I? Well, I reckon I can cure that, all right. Some cold lemonade, mebbe, and a batch of fresh ginger cookies. . . ." She chuckled at their expressions. "Nothin' like a good scare for workin' up an appetite."

With the shotgun tucked comfortably under her arm, Miss Hepatica led the way back down the road to her cabin. Soon they were all sitting around the scrubbed wooden table in Miss Hepatica's tiny kitchen, with the back door open to catch the little breeze that eddied up from the creek nearby.

The lemonade was deliciously tart and icy on their parched throats, the ginger cookies crumbled in their mouths, and as for not eating between meals—well, as Susan whispered to Laurel, you couldn't really call this in between *anything,* could you? It was much more like being on vacation; and they always had different rules for vacations.

When they'd finished the plate of cookies, Miss Hepatica told them to run along outside and play. She and Goldenrod had some gossiping to do.

"Can we go wading in the creek?" Daisy asked.

Goldenrod looked uncertain. "There might be snakes—"

"Or alligators," said Susan. Susan was afraid of only two things in the whole world, alligators (or crocodiles) and the Abominable Snowman, neither of which she had encountered so far.

Miss Hepatica made a high wheezing sound in her throat; it took them a moment to realize she was laughing.

"No alligators, child. Mebbe a water moccasin or two —but they're right bashful."

Her eyes were twinkling again, and they were pretty sure she was only teasing. Still. . . . "I don't know," said Goldenrod in a worried tone. "I wouldn't want to take you home to your mother with any snake bites."

"We'll carry a stick," Heath assured her.

"And the water will help my blister," Daisy said. "You shouldn't take us home with blisters, either, Goldenrod."

"Well—okay." Goldenrod looked at her watch. "But we've got to go pretty soon, so no falling in the water accidentally on purpose. How would I explain *that* to your mother, I'd like to know—bringing you home all soaking wet?"

How were they to get home at all, for that matter? They couldn't help wondering a little about this, but no one asked. Instead they sat down on the back steps to take off their shoes and socks, and then made their way down to the creek.

At first they were content just to wade about in the clear brown water, which felt wonderfully cool on their feet and ankles. But soon Heath became restless and said they ought to explore further. They began picking their way cautiously upstream, with Susan eyeing each dead branch to make sure it really *was* a dead branch. And then Heath spotted the swimming hole.

"Hey!" he said. "A pool!"

A natural dam had been formed by a cluster of rocks with a huge uprooted tree trunk wedged fast among them. Beyond it lay the pool, shining dark and smooth in the slanting late-afternoon sunlight. A big flat rock made a kind of platform along one side.

"I'm going in!" Heath announced, tearing off his shirt and jeans.

"Me, too!" Daisy shucked off her dress.

"Wait a minute!" Laurel glared at them. "You don't know how deep it is, or if it's even safe."

"Other people come here," Val said. He pointed to a length of rope knotted to the limb of an overhanging tree. "It must be okay."

"But Goldenrod said—"

"She said not to fall in," Heath argued. "Well, we're not going to fall in—we're going to jump in!"

Before Laurel could stop him, he had scrambled onto a lower limb of the tree, grasped the rope, and was swinging out over the water. "Here goes nothing!" he yelled, and dropped with a splash. In a moment his face reappeared, grinning.

29

"Come on in!" he yelled. "It's perfect—not too cold, and there isn't any gunk."

Not like the pond where they sometimes swam at home, he meant, where you had to watch out for weeds and mudholes.

"Daisy—!" Laurel began.

But Daisy was already diving from the flat rock. Although she was the youngest, Daisy could already swim like an otter. Laurel wasn't really worried about her, only about what Goldenrod would say.

And yet. . . .

The thought of a swim at the end of this strange, hot afternoon proved too much even for Laurel. Soon they had all plunged into the pool, although Susan studied it carefully first for any suspicious-looking logs. They splashed and shouted and took turns swinging from the rope—all except Val, who was more interested in the dam. Any kind of water system fascinated him; their mother said Val would grow up to be either a plumber or a hydraulic engineer. (Plumbers probably made more money, she added.) He was delicately removing a trapped branch from the spillway in the center of the dam, when a shout from the bank made him look around with a start.

"You kids—you get out of that water this minute!"

It was Goldenrod, her arms full of their shoes and socks. She dumped them onto the ground and stood waiting for them grimly, her fists on her hips. Guiltily, without a word, they swam over to the flat rock and climbed out, dripping.

"Lie down in the sun and dry off," Goldenrod ordered, in a stern baby-sitter's voice. "You realize we have to be home in fifteen minutes? And just look at you!"

They lay down obediently, side by side on the warm rock. For a long time nobody said anything.

"We're sorry, Goldenrod," Heath muttered at last. "We were just going wading, like you said, but then we saw the pool, and—"

"Sure." They heard Goldenrod sigh. "I guess I can't really blame you, not after all the walking I made you do in this heat. It's just that I'm supposed to be in *charge*, see?" After a pause, she said, "How was the water, anyway?"

"Oh, it was super," Susan said drowsily. The mellow rays of the sun still held a surprising heat; she felt her eyelids growing heavy. Somewhere a woodpecker was hammering at a tree, and rich, green smells hung strong and sweet in the warm, still air.

Goldenrod was gathering up their clothes. "Here," she said. "You'd better start putting these back on while I get ready."

They obeyed, wondering what on earth she could mean by "getting ready." If anything, Goldenrod looked as if she were preparing to stay, not go. She had seated herself cross-legged at the foot of the big tree, folding her arms and leaning her head back against the trunk. A dazzle of sunlight caught in her hair and turned it to fiery gold. Laurel saw that her face had gone pale and still, her green eyes narrowed, as if she were thinking hard about something.

Goldenrod glanced around at the children. "Okay? Everybody got their shoes tied? Daisy, you'd better put your sweater back on. And Laurel, don't forget your watch."

They nodded, feeling too sleepy all of a sudden to speak. Slowly Laurel fastened the strap of her watch. It seemed an enormous effort; her hands felt clumsy, her fingers heavy and numb.

"All right," Goldenrod said. "Here we go."

And she tilted back her head and closed her eyes.

Chapter 4 *Some Explanations*

"Oh. . . ." Daisy yawned enormously, stretching in her chair. She felt something tickling the back of her neck and put up a hand to her damp curls.

"Why is my hair all wet?" she asked in a puzzled voice. "Oh, that's right—we went swimming, didn't we? And it was nice," she went on dreamily, "and we didn't even have our bathing suits . . ."

"But how—?" Laurel began.

"Where—?" said Susan.

"What *happened?*" Val demanded. He looked wildly around the living room, at the blaze of October color beyond the windows, at the clock on the mantel that said five minutes to six.

Goldenrod stirred from her position on the couch

and opened her eyes. She stared at the five Madder children, who gazed back at her in bewilderment.

"Oh, my gosh!" she exclaimed, sitting up with a start. "I took you with me, didn't I?"

"To Gorseville," Heath said, nodding soberly. "To look for your friend Pearly."

"Pearly. . . ." Goldenrod repeated, sounding dazed.

She turned her head to stare at the big shoulder bag lying beside her. "That's why," she said slowly. "The letter. I was thinking about Pearly's letter, and about going to Gorseville, and then—"

She broke off. "How was I sitting?" she asked urgently. "Before we left, I mean."

"Well. . . ." Laurel frowned, trying to remember. "You had your arms crossed, and—"

"What about my legs?"

"They were crossed, too," Susan said positively. "And then you closed your eyes, and we thought you were falling asleep, and we felt sleepy, too, and—"

"Oh, my gosh!" Goldenrod said again. She leaned forward and said earnestly, "Look, I'm really sorry. I mean, here I was, supposed to be taking *care* of you, and . . . Is everyone okay?" She sounded anxious.

"I'm sort of tired," Susan admitted. "That was kind of a long walk out to Pearly's. But Miss Hepatica was nice, and the creek was fun."

"And my blister's almost gone," Daisy said reassuringly. "I told you the water would help."

Goldenrod bit her lip. "Of all the dumb things to do —and on my first day, too! But I never took anyone with me before, honestly." She shook her head, frowning. "I just don't see how that could happen."

Heath said, "We had a good time, Goldenrod, really

we did. Being down South and all, and—hey, did you ever find out where Pearly went? Did Miss Hepatica know her address?"

"Kansas City," Goldenrod said and sighed. "I guess I'll never get to see her now."

"Why not?" said Daisy. "We'll go to Kansas City with you if you want, Goldenrod. Only next time maybe we can take a bus, if it's a long way."

"No, no." Goldenrod smiled at them a little sadly. "You don't understand."

"We don't understand *any* of it," Val reminded her. Now that their adventure was over, he was feeling sulky and out of sorts—angry, almost, as though Goldenrod had played some kind of practical joke on them.

"Well. . . ." Goldenrod hesitated.

There was the sound of a car turning into the driveway.

"Here comes your mother. Look," Goldenrod said hurriedly, "I'll explain everything tomorrow, I promise." She stood up. "In the meantime—listen, kids, don't say anything to your mother, okay? About Gorseville, I mean? It was just an accident, anyhow. It won't happen again."

The children stirred uneasily. They weren't used to keeping things from their mother. Oh, little things, maybe, like who lost the good scissors or left their bike out in the rain. But a big thing like this—

"Please," Goldenrod said. Her green eyes were suddenly pleading. "Let me explain first. Then, if you still want to tell her—well, I guess there's nothing I can do about it."

She got her jacket from the closet and slung the strap of the bag over her shoulder. Then she turned back to the children and stopped short. "Oh, my gosh!" she said in dismay. "I forgot—your wet hair!"

Susan said, "It's not really wet any more, just damp. And besides—" She looked at the others, and they nodded slowly; for now, at least, they'd do as Goldenrod asked. "Besides," she said, "Mother probably won't even notice."

And she didn't. In the flurry of putting away the groceries, looking through the mail, and starting supper, Mrs. Madder was almost too busy even to ask how they liked the new sitter.

"She certainly is pretty, isn't she?" she said at the dinner table. "Well, maybe not pretty, exactly, but interesting-looking. . . ." For a moment she pondered Goldenrod's face with her artist's eye. Something odd there, she thought, elusive; *fey,* was that the word she wanted?

"Anyway," she said, looking at the glowing faces of her children around the table, "you all look as if you'd had plenty of fresh air today. In fact, if it wasn't October, I'd say you even got some sunburn. Of course it was a beautiful sunny day, but this late in the year—"

"Well, we *were* outside all afternoon," Heath said truthfully.

"Did Goldenrod go out with you?"

"Oh, yes," Susan said, and Daisy added, "We took a long, long walk."

"Well!" Mrs. Madder looked pleased. "What a relief, to find a sitter who'll actually *do* things with you. Who wants more mashed potatoes?" She served Val's plate and said thoughtfully, "Goldenrod. Such an unusual name; but it suits her, somehow."

"And goldenrod *doesn't* make you sneeze," Susan told her. "That's ragweed."

"Oh, I know. It's too bad more people don't realize that, because goldenrod is such a beautiful plant. There are lots of different varieties, too. People ought to plant it on purpose in their gardens, instead of avoiding it. It would be lovely now in the fall, along with the chrysanthemums and late asters. . . ."

Mrs. Madders' voice trailed off. She was seeing a new picture in her mind—a profusion of flowers, trailing vines, blossoming trees. . . . How odd, she thought. I don't even *like* painting flowers.

Yet when she went up to her attic studio after dinner, she found herself discarding two other paintings she'd been working on, in order to block in the outlines of the new picture. No baby-sitter faces got in the way this time, not even Goldenrod's. She'd be difficult to paint, anyway, Mrs. Madder thought fleetingly: something about her that doesn't come clear. . . .

She looked in some annoyance at the canvas before her. Why *fields,* for heaven's sake? And a cabin? Well, at least the cabin could have a nice quiet color, not like all those garish flowers. Really, Mrs. Madder thought helplessly, picking up her charcoal stick, this isn't my kind of thing at all.

The school hours dragged for the Madder children next day. They could hardly wait to get home and hear Goldenrod's story.

"Maybe she won't come at all," Laurel said anxiously, as she and Val got off the school bus together.

"She'd better," Val said darkly. "Or I'll tell Mother how she kidnaped us."

"Val! You wouldn't! And anyway, she didn't!"

"Well, she just *took* us, didn't she?" he demanded. "Without even asking if we wanted to come."

"But she didn't mean to."

When they turned the corner onto their street, the first thing they saw was Goldenrod's old black Volkswagen parked in front of their house. Goldenrod herself was waiting for them in the living room. She was wearing a yellow shirt with her jeans today, and dangling yellow earrings; but her face looked tired and strained, as if she hadn't slept well the night before.

The first thing she said was: "Now listen, kids—I want you to keep an eye on me today, okay?"

They nodded, puzzled.

"If you notice me starting to cross my arms and my legs both," she told them earnestly, "somebody give a yell. It's much too soon for another trip anyway, and yesterday was just a coincidence, but still—"

"What's a coincidence?" Daisy wanted to know.

"Well—like having two or three things happen at once, sort of by accident, that make something else happen. Like if it hadn't been for Pearly's letter—"

"What *about* Pearly's letter?" Val interrupted. "What's that got to do with anything? I mean, what's so special about some dumb old letter?"

"I said I'd explain," Goldenrod said. "And I will." She met his eyes; Val was the first to look away. "But you may not believe me."

"Oh, we'll believe you," Heath assured her. "We went to Gorseville, didn't we? We just want to know *how.*"

"Well. . . ."

Goldenrod folded her arms and gazed out the window. Susan watched intently to make sure she didn't cross her legs as well.

"Ever since I was a little kid," Goldenrod began slowly, "I've been able to—well, go places. Inside my head, sort of. At least that's how I start out. But they're real places when I get there, and the things that happen really happen."

Thinking of their wet hair and sunburned faces, the children nodded. You couldn't bring back sunburn from a dream, no matter how hot the sun felt.

"I have to be concentrating on the place very hard," Goldenrod went on. "And I have to be sitting in a certain way . . . well, I guess you know about that. And then, when I close my eyes—" She shrugged. "I just go."

Laurel remembered the careful way Goldenrod had arranged herself against the tree trunk by the creek—arms and legs crossed, eyes closed. And her intent face; she must have been concentrating hard on this house, this room, working to bring them back.

"It felt funny," Daisy said, with a frown. "Not bad—just funny."

Heath said in awe, "Can you just go any time you feel like it? And any place you want to?"

Goldenrod shook her head. "No. There are certain rules. Usually I have to wait a couple of weeks, or it doesn't work. Sort of like having a battery recharged, I guess." Val, who understood such things, nodded thoughtfully. "And—well, the other main rule is that I can only get to places that begin with G."

There was a silence, while they all tried to take this in.

"Why just G?" Susan asked at last.

"Because my name begins with a G, I guess." Goldenrod shrugged. "Anyhow, that's the way it works—don't ask me why."

Daisy said wisely, "And that's why we can't go to Kansas City."

Goldenrod nodded. "Gorseville was one thing, but—oh, if I only hadn't been too late!"

She sighed. "See, what happened yesterday was I suddenly remembered Pearly's letter that I'd been carrying around with me—you know, meaning to answer it when I had time. And then I got to thinking about Gorseville, the way Pearly described it, and how it had been a long time since I took one of my trips. I guess I was sort of tired to begin with, and it felt so good to be sitting down, and . . ." She shrugged again. "Well, off we went. Though how you kids happened to come along beats me."

"Gosh!" Heath's eyes were blazing with excitement. "You mean if you'd been thinking about—well, let's see . . ." He searched his mind for places beginning with *G* "If you'd been thinking about Guatemala, say, would we have gone there instead?"

"Well . . ." Goldenrod looked uncertain. "I don't know much about Guatemala. I have to have a picture of the place in my mind before I can go there. That's what I mean about concentrating. I guess Gorseville wasn't too exciting," she said apologetically.

"But listen!" Heath was almost stammering in his eagerness. "What about *us?* I mean, we got to go with you once—maybe we can learn to do it, too! Like if I started concentrating on a place beginning with *H—*"

"I don't think it would work," Goldenrod said. "At least I never heard of anyone else who could do it. It's just something you're born with, I guess."

But Heath had already crossed his arms and legs, closed his eyes, and screwed his face into an expression of fierce concentration.

"Heath!" Laurel said in alarm. Heaven only knew

where they might wind up if Heath decided to go traveling.

"Hey!" Val protested. "Kenny's coming over in a while to play ball. I don't want to go anywhere today!"

"*Sshh!*" said Susan.

They all watched Heath anxiously. Daisy took a tight grip on the arms of her chair, just in case.

But nothing happened. Heath opened his eyes at last, looked around, and said, "Darn!"

Susan asked with interest, "Where were you trying to get to?"

"Hawaii," Heath answered disappointedly.

"Well, I'm glad we didn't go," Daisy said. "We'd really need our bathing suits there. *And* the sunburn cream."

"Yeah, and my snorkel and flippers," Val put in, in spite of himself.

But Heath had a new idea. "What if you helped?" he demanded, turning to Goldenrod. "I mean, what if you concentrated *with* us?"

"Yes—what about that, Goldenrod?" Susan was almost as excited as Heath. "Maybe it would work if you'd start us off."

"Well, I don't know," Goldenrod said doubtfully. "I never tried it before."

"You never took anyone else along before, either," Heath pointed out. "And think of all the places we could go, with all our different names! You wouldn't be stuck with just G places any more. Come on, Goldenrod, couldn't we just *try?*"

He looked at her pleadingly, and Susan said, "Yes! Oh, please, Goldenrod!"

Val said, "Stop pestering her, will you? Maybe she

41

needs time to think about it." He had noticed that Gold-enrod was looking increasingly troubled and uneasy.

But all she said was, "Well, we couldn't go anywhere today, anyhow. It's much too soon."

The she stood up and said in an ordinary baby-sitter's voice: "Okay, everybody—who wants to help me make an apple pie for supper? I got some free apples from the store. Kind of bruised," she explained, "but they'll be all right for pie."

"With whipped cream on top?" Daisy asked. Daisy would eat almost anything with whipped cream on top—even things like squash and rhubarb.

"Sure. Who's good at making pie crust?"

"I am," said Susan—which was irritating, but true.

Val punched his catcher's mitt with his fist and gave Goldenrod a quick, shy glance. "I was hoping maybe you could come out and play ball with us for a while. I mean, if you feel like it."

"As soon as we finish the pie," Goldenrod told him, and gave him one of her rare smiles. "But hey—what about homework, you kids? I don't want your mom to think I'm letting you goof off every afternoon."

Laurel sighed. It was just as well they hadn't gone to Hawaii, she thought. Another whole chapter to read for social studies, and all those French verbs to memorize. . . .

"I'll do mine when I get back," Heath said, and let himself quickly out the front door. He waited for Gold-enrod to call. "Where are you going?" the way Miss Vetch always had; but she didn't. He got on his bike and rode off down the street, heading for a part of town where some new houses were going up. One of the work-men had been a ship's carpenter in his youth; sometimes he talked to Heath while he worked, telling stories about all the foreign ports and people he'd seen.

But today this prospect didn't seem as fascinating as usual. As he pedaled through the familiar streets, it occurred to Heath that even if his idea didn't work, there were still plenty of exciting G places they could go, if Goldenrod would only take them. Greece, for instance, or Greenland, or the Galapagos Islands; or the Golden Gate in San Francisco. Heath didn't care much for cities, but he'd always wanted to walk across the Golden Gate Bridge.

Chapter 5 Val's Trip

They decided that Val should be the first to try. As even Heath had to admit, Val was the best of them all at concentrating. Whether he was playing baseball or reading a book or just sailing twigs down a stream, nothing ever distracted Val. Their mother said he was like a mole at times, blind to anything but the particular tunnel he was digging.

But Val was not enthusiastic. For one thing, he was sure the idea wouldn't work, even if Goldenrod agreed to help. For another, he couldn't think of any place he wanted to go. As fast as the others made suggestions, he turned them down.

"Venezuela?" said Heath.

"Vermont?" said Susan. "That's not even very far."

But Val shook his head stubbornly.

"Oh, come on, Val, just think of a place!" Laurel said in exasperation.

It was a Saturday morning, and they were all up in the boys' room. Mrs. Madder had gone down to the public library to look up pictures of magnolia trees, for some reason; but they were keeping the door shut, just in case. Without actually putting it into words, the children had decided not to say anything to their mother just yet. Time enough for that, they all felt, if the thing really worked.

"Vancouver?" said Heath. He flopped over onto his back on the rug and gazed at the ceiling, trying to think of more *V* places. "Valley Forge?"

"Look," Val protested. "I don't really want to go *anywhere!* There's enough things to do around here without wasting a whole afternoon in some strange place where I woudn't even know anybody and there wouldn't be anything to do."

"Oh, Val!" they groaned.

Daisy said, "How about Verner Falls?" and everybody groaned again. Verner Falls was a neighboring town where Daisy's friend Heather lived. "Well," she said defensively, "at least you'd know Heather. And her brother has an electric train set, so there would too be something to do."

"Vienna," Heath was muttering to himself. "Victoria, Valparaiso—that's in Chile, I think—"

"Venice!" Laurel exclaimed, so loudly that they all jumped. "That's it—Venice!"

She had been staring at the row of maps lining Heath's side of the room. Now she pointed excitedly to the map of Europe.

"You'd like Venice, Val—all those canals!"

45

"Canals?" Val's face brightened.

"Sure, they have canals instead of streets, and those boats—gondolas, they're called—"

"Where's Venice?" Daisy wanted to know.

"In Italy. Gosh, I wonder if Goldenrod knows how to talk Italian," Laurel said, thinking that her French verbs weren't likely to do them much good in Italy, even if she managed to learn them all between now and next week.

"Hey—Italy!" Susan said. "Pizza and spaghetti and lasagna . . . you love lasagna, Val," she added encouragingly.

But Val was already intrigued by the thought of the canals. He studied the map, seeing how Venice sat out on a point by itself in a patch of blue—the Adriatic Sea, the map said.

Heath said dreamily, "And there are bridges and old, old churches and pictures and a big square with pigeons . . ."

Heath never forgot anything he read or saw about a foreign place. Soon they were all talking at once, deciding just what they'd do when they got to Venice. Val reminded them that they still had to persuade Goldenrod to help them; but looking at his eager face and glowing eyes, the others didn't think that would be much of a problem.

And it wasn't—at least not the idea of the trip itself. But Goldenrod balked at the idea of Venice.

"It's like I told you," she said. "I have to know something about a place before I can go there. I never was much good at history, and . . . well, I never even *tried* to go any place fancy like Europe. I might get it all wrong," she explained.

Wrong? They stared at her, wondering what she meant. Then Laurel remembered something about their trip to Gorseville that had puzzled her at the time.

"When we were down South," she said. "The way all the trees and flowers were blooming at once—and all the different crops they were raising—I mean, there were pink dogwood trees in the woods, but the corn was ripe, too!"

She stopped expectantly; but Goldenrod looked blank.

"Well, dogwoods flower in the spring," Laurel explained. "And I'm pretty sure magnolias do, too. But then what about the corn and the pumpkins and those great big sunflowers? And I think you have to be really way down South to raise sugar cane—"

"Yeah, well, I'm not so hot on all that stuff," Goldenrod said apologetically. "I just thought . . . oh, you know, down South things ought to look pretty and smell good and everything. I mean, as long as I get the *place* right, I figure the details don't matter too much."

Susan frowned, but Daisy said loyally, "Well, I don't care, Goldenrod, I thought it was just right. And when we get to Venice—"

Goldenrod sighed. "Look, kids—forget Venice, can't you? Pick someplace easier. You know, someplace *ordinary.*"

"But that's the only place Val wants to go," Susan told her.

Laurel had an idea. "I'll get the encyclopedia," she said. "You can real all about Venice in there. And maybe there'll be some pictures, too."

She found the heavy volume marked *V* and gave it to Goldenrod. Meanwhile Heath remembered a painting of Venice he'd seen in one of his mother's art books, and went up to the studio to get it.

"Hey, it looks kind of nice," Goldenrod admitted after a while, turning pages. "These boatmen characters with the ribbons in their hats and guitars, or whatever they are—"

She broke off to stare at the picture Heath was holding up for her to see. It was a shimmer of light in which the shapes of masts and sails and towers and bridges all seemed to be floating in a kind of golden haze. Even the water appeared to be condensing into a mist of colored reflections. The picture was signed by a man named Turner.

"Hey, I don't want to go there in a *fog!*" Goldenrod objected.

"Well, it was just to give you an idea," Heath said. "And at least it's in color, not like the pictures in the book. I mean, we wouldn't want to go to a place like Venice in black and white."

"We won't," Goldenrod assured him. "If we go there at all."

But she agreed finally that Venice was worth a try, and they settled on a day for the trip. There were practical things to decide, too, like what to wear and how much money to take. "I bet they don't let you ride in those crazy boats for free," Goldenrod observed. Val insisted he had plenty of allowance saved up; Goldenrod shouldn't have to pay, he said, since she was the one who'd be doing most of the work.

As for clothes—well, nobody really knew what Venice was like at this time of year. Certainly not as hot as Gorseville, they agreed, but probably warmer than here

48

at home, and damper. They decided on light sweaters and windbreakers; and sneakers, in case they did a lot of walking.

Everyone except Val was in a fever of excitement for days beforehand—so much so that their mother wondered if they could be coming down with the flu. Val himself never thought much about the future, being too absorbed in whatever he happened to be doing at the moment. Still, when the great day came, he found himself feeling unexpectedly nervous; even a little scared.

They took up their positions around the living room, trying to sit exactly as they had on the day of the Gorseville trip. Goldenrod crossed her arms and legs and closed her eyes, and Val followed suit—crossing his fingers, too, for good measure. Part of his mind still refused to believe that anything at all would happen; the other part couldn't help thinking how far away Venice was, and what if they never got back home again? But he squeezed his eyes tight shut and forced himself to start concentrating.

"Wait!" said Goldenrod.

They all jumped, and Val opened his eyes quickly. Nothing had happened yet, he saw with some relief, except that it was beginning to rain outside.

"We'd better be concentrating on the same place—the same part of Venice," Goldenrod explained. "We don't want to get separated."

"The Grand Canal?" Val suggested, remembering the picture in the encyclopedia. "In a gondola?"

"No, that might be kind of dangerous. Like if we arrived too suddenly, the thing might tip over." She considered a moment. "How about that big square—the one with the church and the pigeons?"

49

"St. Mark's." Val nodded. "Okay," he said, although his throat felt dry. "Let's both concentrate on that."

They closed their eyes again. In the silence they could hear a car swishing by on the wet street outside, and Mrs. Teasel next door calling her cat in out of the rain. "Here, kitty! Here, kitty-kitty-kitty. . . ."

Laurel suppressed a giggle. This is crazy, she thought, it's completely nutty—why, there's a whole ocean between us and Venice! If I'm feeling a little sleepy (she yawned hugely) , it's only because of sitting around the house in my outdoor clothes. Mother always says not to, it's bad for your circulation, and besides—besides. . . .

A tremendous whirring sound startled them. They opened their eyes. Pigeons, hundreds of them, were rising in a great fan against a tattered blue sky. Somewhere a band was playing. And straight ahead of them rose an enormous building, all marble and colored pictures, whose gold domes flashed and glittered in the windy sunshine.

"We did it!" Val said in awe. "We're here!"

"The Piazza San Marco," Goldenrod agreed. She gazed around in satisfaction at the huge square lined with shops and cafes, bustling with people; at the tall bell tower, looking exactly as the encyclopedia had pictured it; and at the great cathedral dominating the scene, whose size and splendor the pictures had only suggested.

Then she turned to the children and said, in a practical baby-sitter's voice, "Well, it's a good thing we brought our windbreakers, anyway. Daisy, stand still for a minute so I can tie your hood."

Daisy was jumping up and down, laughing in sheer delight. Laurel stood transfixed by the scene before her, like nothing she had ever imagined. Heath nudged her and said, "Those people—that family that just went by —they were talking Italian!"

"Well, what did you expect?" Laurel came out of her trance in time to stop him from racing off across the square in his excitement. "We've got to stick together," she told him, grabbing his sleeve firmly. "This is a whole *city*, Heath, and we've only got a few hours to be here."

"What'll we do first?" demanded Susan—orderly Susan, always wanting to make a plan.

"The dungeons!" said Heath. He pointed to the great stone bulk of the Doge's Palace to the right of the cathedral, and the Bridge of Sighs leading from it to the ancient prison.

"The water!" said Val. "The Grand Canal's right over there, I remember from the pictures."

"The cathedral!" said Laurel. "I want to see the inside."

"The glasses!" said Daisy. "They make glasses here, the book said so. They take a funny-looking pipe, and then they blow and blow and—"

"Oh, Daisy, that's off on some island somewhere," Susan told her. "We won't have time for that."

As Daisy's eyes began to fill with tears, Goldenrod said firmly, "The first thing we're all going to do is have some hot chocolate. We need something warm inside us before we start, especially if we're going out on the water. Val's choice comes first," she said, over the others' protests. "After all, he helped get us here, didn't he?"

Nobody was going to argue against food at any rate, especially between meals; and they found a corner cafe sheltered from the wind by gaily striped awnings.

"*Grazie,*" said Goldenrod to the waiter, who obligingly pushed two tables together to make room for them all. He smiled and said something to her in rapid Italian. To the children's astonishment, she replied in the same language—slowly and haltingly, to be sure; but the waiter seemed to understand her. He nodded and went away to fill their orders.

"Gosh, Goldenrod—I didn't know you knew Italian," Val exclaimed.

"I didn't, either," Goldenrod said, looking puzzled.

Their chocolate came steaming, with swirls of whipped cream on top, which made Daisy forget her disappointment about Murano, the glassmakers' island. She could see some of the glass in the shops here, Laurel pointed out; and maybe, if it wasn't too expensive, they could buy a small piece of it to take home.

"No," Goldenrod said sharply. "You can't take anything back with you. That's one of the rules. Otherwise—" she hesitated. "Well, anyhow, that's just the way it is."

Laurel remembered the doll in Gorseville, lying abandoned in Pearly's driveway—how Goldenrod had picked it up and then slowly put it down again. For a moment she felt sad, without knowing why. Then the voices of the others recalled her to the gay and brilliant scene. Venice, Italy, on an ordinary Thursday afternoon! And for once she didn't even have any homework to worry about.

They finished their hot chocolate, and Val paid for it. There was an anxious moment when they wondered if the waiter would accept their American money; but he did. "Money is money in any language, I guess," Goldenrod said. Then they set off in different directions to explore the square, Val having generously decided to allow everyone a free half-hour before they took to the water.

While he and Heath made for the Doges' Palace, Laurel and Susan wandered about inside the cathedral. They marveled at the great mosaic pictures—like giant jigsaw puzzles, as Susan said; it was the kind of project that appealed to her. Meanwhile Goldenrod took Daisy on a tour of the shops. There was the famous Venetian glass, glowing with all the colors of the rainbow—and tapestries, too, and woodcarvings, and lace as fine as a spider's web. "A very *smart* spider," Daisy said in awe.

At the end of the half-hour, they met back at the cafe and left the bright windy spaces of the great square behind them, in search of a gondola to hire. Soon they were wandering through a bewildering maze of shadowy streets with tall, narrow houses. There were small squares here, with churches and shops and cafes, each neighborhood linked to the next by the graceful stone bridges that spanned the green waters of the canals.

"Streets!" Val said in disgust. "I didn't think they had streets—I thought it was all canals."

"Well, it's nice to be able to go to the store without having to get into a *boat* every time you need a loaf of bread or something," Susan told him.

They were coming to yet another bridge.

"Oh, look!" said Daisy, stopping short at the edge of the canal.

A long black gondola with curving prows, like some exotic sea bird, was gliding to a stop alongside them. The young gondolier leaned on his oar, smiling up at them, and made a graceful, sweeping gesture at the cushioned seats of his craft. He was wearing an ordinary turtlenecked sweater and a thick knitted cap—but if

53

Goldenrod was disappointed not to find him in costume, she didn't show it.

She smiled back and said something to him in Italian; and after a short discussion, they were all climbing down in to the gently rocking gondola.

"Careful!" Goldenrod reached out to steady Heath. "He says we're really too many for his boat—but if Daisy sits on my lap, it'll be okay."

Daisy started to object, but thought better of it. The gondolier flashed them another smile, and pushed off. In a few minutes they had left the shadowed, murky waters of the small canal behind and were emerging into the sun and wind once more, out onto the choppy blue expanse of the Grand Canal.

"Barber poles!" Susan exclaimed, pointing at the shoreline. "Why do they need so many barbers?"

Goldenrod repeated this to the gondolier, who threw back his head and laughed.

"He says they're mooring poles for people's boats," Goldenrod explained. "Some of them have the family colors painted on them."

"You mean people *live* in those places?" Laurel stared at the magnificent palaces lining the shore, some of them almost as lavishly decorated with gold and mosaics as the cathedral itself.

Val was sitting in the bow, raptly taking in all the busy water traffic of the Grand Canal. Small motor launches darted from shore to shore, weaving in and out of smaller vessels—excursion boats, sailboats, prosaic barges.

"Look!" Heath said suddenly. He was facing west into the sun, which flared low in the sky now, striking a dazzle of reflections from the water, so that the whole city seemed to tremble in its radiance. "That's what the painting was about," he explained; but no one else knew what he meant.

Goldenrod had been talking to the handsome gondolier—who, Laurel noticed, was doing his best to flirt with her. He kept flashing his smile and gazing romantically into her eyes. But Goldenrod was having none of it. Although her Italian seemed to become swifter and more fluent each time she spoke, her manner remained as cool and practical as ever. Now she glanced at her watch and nodded; and the gondola turned back for shore.

"Oh, no! Not already!" the children protested.

"This is expensive, for one thing," Goldenrod told them. "And for another, Daisy's getting wet." It was true that Daisy, sitting higher than the rest of them, had received most of the spray from the choppy waves and the wakes of other boats—not that she seemed to mind.

"Anyhow, it's getting late. But he'll let us off right here on the Grand Canal so we can see the sunset. He says there's going to be a beautiful one tonight."

As the gondolier steered them expertly through the small craft crowding the shoreline, all the bells of the city began to ring at once—or so it seemed. From bell tower after bell tower, the peals rang out, almost drowning out the whine of the motor launches and the cries of sea gulls that dipped and soared above the water.

And now the sun was setting. By the time the gondolier (with a last lingering glance at Goldenrod) had left them at a small stone landing stage, long scarves of cloud were drifting across the sky . . . blue and orange, lavender and green and rose. The domes and towers of Venice, the pastel walls and marble balustrades, all glowed in the mellow light as if lit from within.

"It's like a city in a dream," Susan said in a hushed voice.

"Well, that's all it will be in a few minutes," Goldenrod reminded them briskly. "Take a good look, everybody, because it's almost time to go home."

"Hey!" Val had been standing at the very edge of the landing stage, where small waves lapped at the mossy stones. Now he pointed at his feet and said, "The water—it's rising!"

They stared. Sure enough, water was slowly flooding the platform on which they stood, beginning to lick at the toes of their sneakers. Maybe it was just the tide . . . but did tides ever happen this fast?

Laurel cried, "It's not rising—we're sinking!"

They looked around in horror. Gently but steadily, the whole magnificent shoreline was sliding down into the sunset-streaked waters of the Grand Canal. And now their sneakers were wet, the water was rising around their ankles . . .

"Quick!" said Goldenrod. "Everybody move back. Val, come here!"

A narrow stone ledge projected from the building behind them. Goldenrod propped herself against it, crossing her arms and legs as best she could, closing her eyes. Val copied her gingerly, scared his feet would slide out from under him. It was an effort to make himself close his eyes against the rising tide of water.

"Home," Goldenrod said urgently. "Think of home, Val, as hard as you can!"

Chapter 6 Some Decisions

"I want to go home!" Daisy whimpered . . . and opened her eyes.

Val and Goldenrod were sitting side by side on the green couch opposite her. Heath and Susan occupied the armchairs on either side of the fireplace; Laurel sat on the straight chair near the window.

They stared at one another. For a moment nobody moved, as if afraid to test the reality of the familiar room around them.

"Here kitty-kitty-kitty!" Mrs. Teasel was calling her cat again, for supper this time. They could just hear the faint shrilling of her voice above the rain that drummed against the windowpanes.

"Wow!" Heath said shakily. "What happened, anyway?"

"Oh, poor Venice!" Susan, who rarely cried, sounded on the verge of tears. *"We're* all right—but Venice—and all the people, and the beautiful buildings—"

"Do you think it's all gone by now?" Daisy asked in awe. "Could a whole city just *drown* like that?"

"Wait a minute," Laurel said slowly. She looked at Goldenrod. "The book said Venice was sinking, didn't it?"

Goldenrod nodded, running trembling fingers through her hair. She looked pale and distraught. "If I'd known how dangerous it was going to be—"

Laurel interrupted. "Goldenrod, it's not sinking *fast!* An inch or two every ten years, that's all, and nowadays they have engineers working on it—"

"Sure," said Val, coming out of his daze. "It's because the city's not really built on land, it's built on mud, and they have to keep shoring it up."

"The book said sinking," Goldenrod insisted. She met the accusing gaze of the children and clapped a hand to her mouth. "Oh, my gosh!" she said. "I did it again, didn't I? I told you I wasn't so good about details—"

"Details!" Susan exclaimed angrily. "We could have been drowned. And what about Venice?"

"Venice is still there," Laurel told her. She began to smile. "Just the way Gorseville is still there, even if the magnolias aren't out in October, or the dogwoods, or—" But she was laughing too hard to go on.

For a moment the others just stared at her. Then they all began laughing—even Goldenrod, who so rarely even smiled.

"Oh, how dumb can you get?" she sighed at last, leaning weakly back against the couch. "Next time you kids make sure I read the fine print, will you?" Then her tone changed. "But hey, look—your mother will be home any time now, and what about your wet sneakers? They're making puddles on the rug."

This struck them funny all over again. Heath laughed so hard he choked and had to be pounded on the back by Susan.

"In the dryer!" said Goldenrod. "Quick—everybody put their sneakers in the dryer while I mop up the rug."

"We'll just say we went for a walk," Susan objected. "That's what we said last time, after we went to Gorseville. And the way it's raining outside—"

"What kind of a sitter takes kids out walking in the rain?" Goldenrod demanded. "Without their boots on, even? Now come on, off with the shoes and socks."

They obeyed reluctantly, peeling off their wet sneakers and socks and padding barefoot into the kitchen to toss them into the dryer. But their mood had sobered. When Goldenrod said, "Okay, now—upstairs and put on dry shoes," they hesitated. "Well, go on!" she said impatiently.

Heath spoke for them all. "We don't like lying to our mother," he said.

The others nodded. Goldenrod looked at their stubborn faces. "But . . ."

"Anyway, I don't think she'd mind," Laurel said earnestly. "About our trips, I mean. She always wanted to travel, only she never had enough money, and now, with all of us kids—"

"She would have loved Venice," Susan put in. "Except for the sinking part. And she wouldn't even have minded that very much—Mother likes things to happen."

Daisy said eagerly, "Maybe she could come with us next time. Could she, Goldenrod?"

Goldenrod's face closed up. That was the only way Val could think to describe it. The green eyes went cloudy, her mouth lost its curve. She regarded them for a moment without expression; then turned away wordlessly.

Bewildered, they followed her back into the living room, where she silently put on her jacket and slung her bag over her shoulder. She checked her watch, and then stood gazing out the window into the rainy dusk with her arms folded, like someone waiting for a bus. She didn't look angry, just distant, as though she had already traveled miles away from them.

"Goldenrod?" Heath said uncertainly.

Daisy said, "You're coming back, aren't you, Goldenrod? Tomorrow, I mean?" She looked anxiously up at Goldenrod's face.

"I guess not." Goldenrod's voice sounded as remote as she looked. "If you kids want to tell your mother— well, I can't stop you. But in that case, I'll have to be leaving."

"Leaving?" Val said. "Leaving town, you mean?"

"Probably." She shrugged. "There'll be questions, and . . . well, never mind all that. I'd probably lose my job, anyhow. The minute people find out you're some kind of a freak—"

"But Mother wouldn't tell anyone!" Susan protested. "She can be just as secret as we can. And she wouldn't think you were a freak, Goldenrod. I mean, *we* certainly don't think so, and—"

"Different," Goldenrod said. "A freak, a nut. Maybe

I'm a witch, even." She shrugged again. "Or on drugs, more likely."

"But Mother wouldn't—" Heath began in horror.

"No. People don't understand," Goldenrod told them in a toneless voice. "Kids, maybe, but not grown-ups. Not parents. Parents least of all."

"But—"

"I'm sorry, kids."

She glanced at her watch again, and they saw there was no use arguing with her. She looked so lonely, Val thought, standing there staring out into the rain. No, not lonely; *alone*. . . .

The children exchanged troubled glances. When they heard the sound of their mother's car turning into the driveway, they hesitated—but only for a moment.

"Come on!" Laurel said. "Dry shoes, everybody!"

Goldenrod turned. Her green eyes widened. They grinned at her. Slowly her shoulders relaxed; the life came back into her face. She gave a little sigh and smiled back at them. There was apology as well as relief in the smile.

"See you tomorrow, Goldenrod," they yelled, and raced for the stairs.

At the last minute, Laurel grabbed an armful of laundry from the bathroom hamper, took the sneakers out of the drier and dumped the whole load into the washing machine with a cupful of soap. Their sneakers could use washing, anyway, and even if their mother didn't notice the damp spots on the rug, she was bound to hear the dryer thumping away and wonder how they'd all managed to get their feet so wet, rain or no rain.

It was Val who finally put the seal on their silence.

"If we didn't have Goldenrod," he pointed out, "we might have to have Miss Vetch back again. And you know how Mother would feel about *that*."

As a matter of fact, Mrs. Rose Madder was feeling happier about her household these days than she had in years. The children were bright-eyed and healthy; and it seemed to her there were fewer arguments and fights. Daisy was more independent, less given to whining and wheedling now that Miss Vetch was no longer around to baby her. Val didn't sulk as much, and Susan seemed less bossy. Laurel invited her friends over to the house more often to giggle and gossip; the worried expression had left her eyes. Heath continued to roam the town in his spare time—but now he entertained them all at dinner with stories of the people and places he'd seen.

And Mrs. Madder herself felt less tired in the evenings, even though there was more to do. She cooked things she and the children liked, and never mind if some of the meals weren't particularly well-balanced or came straight from the freezer. ("Frozen pizza is not a meal in *my* cookbook," Miss Vetch had been fond of saying in her twinkly way.) And if she'd had an especially exhausting day, Mrs. Madder could kick off her shoes and lie down on the couch after dinner with a book, with no Miss Vetch to reproach her by busily knitting or darning in the chair opposite.

Even her painting was going well. She'd almost finished the flower picture, which was turning out better than she'd expected—splashy, but quite effective. Now she had a new idea for a painting of birds. Pigeons, they would be; not that she was terribly fond of pigeons, but somehow pigeons kept insisting themselves to her. It would be a bright, breezy picture, with rags of color flying across it, and a glitter of sunlight on gold . . . Gold? Mrs. Madder couldn't think why or how this particular idea had come to her; but then, that was often the way with her paintings.

If the children's consciences still bothered them a little, they forgot it in the excitement of planning Laurel's trip. They'd drawn straws this time, and Laurel had gotten the short one. No one minded; they all felt sure that Laurel would be bound to choose a reasonable kind of place where nothing too dramatic could happen. After Venice, they were ready for a quiet, peaceful kind of trip.

Laurel thought for a few days, and then announced that she knew where she wanted to go: Laramie, Wyoming.

"I had a hard time deciding against London," she said with a sigh. "But we've already been to one big city, and —well, I've always wanted to go out West, especially Wyoming."

They'd promised not to argue, but—

"Horses!" Val said in disgust. "That's what it is, Goldenrod. She's horse crazy."

"I am not!"

They were all outside in the backyard, raking leaves under Goldenrod's direction. Laurel's pink cheeks turned even pinker as Val persisted.

"She is too," he told Goldenrod. "All because she had a couple of riding lessons last summer on some old nag—"

"I had ten lessons, and Clover *wasn't* a nag, she was part Arabian and part Morgan and very high-spirited!"

"And about twenty years old."

63

"Twenty isn't all that old for a horse," Laurel said angrily. "A lot you know about it!"

She started after Val with her rake, and Val dodged behind a maple tree. Laurel hardly ever lost her temper, but when she did, the others respected it.

"Hey!" Goldenrod grabbed her arm. "Listen, Laurel, if you want to go to—where was it again?"

"Laramie."

"Laramie, that's where we'll go. Just don't expect to get me on a horse, though. I'm scared of horses. Daisy," she called, "here's another pile for you."

Daisy dragged the big plastic bag across the yard and held it open while Heath scooped armfuls of leaves into it. "You said we could leave one pile for jumping in," she reminded Goldenrod.

"Listen, there are still about two million leaves left," Heath said glumly. He'd planned on a long bike ride this afternoon, out to an old quarry where you could pretend you were maybe a prospector or a rock climber or miles from civilization. "I don't see why Laurel can't choose someplace more interesting. Like Lapland, where the reindeer are, or Lima—that's in Peru—"

"Or Loch Lomond," said Daisy, who had been learning the song in school.

"Yeah. Or Loch Ness. Hey, what about that?" Heath's blue eyes shone. "Maybe we'd get to see the monster!"

"There isn't any monster," Susan told him briskly, raking a pile of leaves over to the bag. "That's just a silly legend."

"Oh, that's what you think, smarty! Listen, they've got a whole bunch of scientists over there studying it, they wouldn't be wasting their time if—"

"Hand me your rake, will you, Heath?" said Goldenrod, seeing another fight coming on. She began prying
leaves from the bottom of the prickly hedge that separated the Madders' property from Mrs. Teasel's next
door. "Like I said, you kids—if Laurel wants to go to
Laramie, that's where we're going, and no more arguing. What kind of place is it, anyway, Laurel?"

"Well—" Laurel began.

"It's just an ordinary town," Val said, rejoining them
and snatching up his rake. He was mad because he'd
wanted to go to the Great Lakes. Lake Superior, Lake
Ontario—any one of them would have done. "Laurel
thinks it's all cowboys and Indians like in some corny
Western, but that was a long time ago. They have cars
and buses and office buildings just like any place else.
Laramie! I ask you."

Laurel took a deep breath and tried to speak calmly.

"Look, Laramie's just a place to start from. We're
not going to *stay* there. It's the ranches I want to get to,
and the grazing land, and the mountains. . . ." Her face
grew dreamy. Laurel had read *Green Grass of Wyoming*
three times in the past year.

"Mountains," Heath said, cheering up. "The Rockies.
The Tetons and the Bighorns and the Medicine Bow—"

"Anyhow," Laurel went on, "we need an *L* place to
begin with. That's why I thought of Laramie. Maybe we
could arrive on the very edge of town and then start
walking," she added, with an uncertain look at Goldenrod.

Goldenrod straightened up, brushing the bright hair
back from her eyes, and leaned on her rake, considering.

"I don't know," she said. "It might be kind of a long

walk to anywhere. Like the West is a pretty big place, you know—things aren't right next door to each other, the way they are here."

Susan was attacking another pile of leaves over by the garage. Now she looked up and said, "Why couldn't we get a car?"

They all stared at her.

"Well," she said reasonably, "it seems to me if we can get to these places at all, we could have a car waiting for us. Just to borrow, I mean." She thought for a moment. "If Laurel and Goldenrod both concentrated on a car somebody just happened to leave their keys in—and they wouldn't be needing it for a couple of hours—"

"A truck would be even better," Goldenrod said, narrowing her green eyes thoughtfully. "Like if it's rough country—and with six of us—"

"But that would be stealing!" Heath said, wide-eyed, and Daisy asked simultaneously, "Can you drive a truck, Goldenrod?"

"Oh, sure," Goldenrod said casually. "And it wouldn't be stealing," she assured Heath. "Not *bad* stealing, anyway, if we fixed it the way Susan said. You kids," she marveled. "You really come up with some wild ideas! With all the trips I've taken, I never even thought of that. A car!"

A chill wind had sprung up, rustling the big pile of leaves at the end of the yards and spinning a few more down from the almost-bare branches of the trees.

Goldenrod said, "Hey, we'd better get the rest of these leaves picked up, or we'll have to start raking all over again." She shivered. "I hope it won't be too cold out in Wyoming this time of year. Well, at least we know what to wear—jeans and sweaters. And everybody speaks English."

Daisy, who was dragging the big bag down to the end of the yard, paused and said, "But you talked okay in Venice, Goldenrod."

"That's right—I did, didn't I?" Goldenrod shook her head. "Crazy! I couldn't talk a word of Italian now if my life depended on it."

That evening, as they were undressing for bed, Laurel said to Susan, "I just hope Goldenrod gets all the details right this time."

"She sounded like she's been out West before. And I don't see exactly what she could get *wrong*. I mean, if it's just going to be a lot of cows and grass and some old mountains—"

Susan shrugged. She too was feeling disgruntled; truck or no truck, the whole trip still sounded much too vague and unplanned for Susan's taste.

"Well, California's the West, too. I just hope we don't wind up in the middle of a bunch of palm trees or stuck off in a desert somewhere." Laurel finished brushing her hair and drew it back into a ponytail for the night. She said thoughtfully, "I wonder if that's where Goldenrod's from. Originally, I mean."

"California?"

"Oh—just the West. Someplace far away. I mean, I get the feeling she doesn't know anyone around here, and . . ." Laurel paused uneasily. "Well, it's almost as if she's hiding from somebody. Do you think maybe she ran away from home?"

"Goldenrod wouldn't need to run away," Susan pointed out. "She could just *go*."

"But only for a few hours. At least. . . ." Laurel

67

shook her head, baffled; her hair gave a switch like the tail of a real pony. "Well, anyway—what she said about grown-ups and parents. Something really bad must have happened to her once, don't you think? And the way she never stays very long in one place, as if she didn't trust people, or—"

"Maybe it's just the way she is," Susan said, getting into bed and drawing the covers up neatly under her chin. "Like Heath. Look at the way *he* moves around. Goldenrod practically had to sit on him before he'd stay home today and help with the leaves."

"But Heath likes to see new places and meet people and get involved; and Goldenrod. . . ."

Laurel shook her head again. She couldn't explain exactly what she meant. But it occurred to her, just as she was falling asleep, that none of them really knew any more now about Goldenrod than they had the day she arrived. Laurel wondered if they ever would.

Chapter 7 Laurel's Trip

"For Pete's sake!" said Val, staring at the truck. "Couldn't you do any better than *that?*"

The truck was a battered pickup that had once been painted blue. Now it was mostly rust-colored and had a sag in the middle, like an old horse. It stood forlornly at the edge of the highway—the only man-made object to be seen in all this vast Wyoming world of grass and sky.

"I wasn't concentrating on the *kind* of truck," Goldenrod said defensively. "Just so it was about the right size and had the keys in it. It does look pretty beat-up," she admitted.

"Well, I don't care." Laurel took a deep, exhilarating breath of the clear air. It smelled of mint and sage and sweet grass; more than that, she thought, it smelled of the West itself. "We're here," she said happily, "and that's all that matters."

"But *where* are we?" Susan demanded, gazing around in dismay. "Where's Laramie?"

"We said the edge of town," Heath reminded her.

"But this isn't the edge of anywhere!" Susan turned about in a circle to stare at the horizon. Mountains and more mountains, making a jagged frame around the immense blue sky. "Where are all the houses and the people? I don't even see any cows!"

"Cattle," Laurel told her. "Out here you don't call them *cows*, Susan!"

Goldenrod said cheerfully, "Well, that's why we've got the truck—so we can go exploring."

She wrenched open the door of the cab, which almost came off in her hands, and settled herself on the peeling upholstery to try the ignition. The old truck gave a series of horrible racking coughs and then shuddered into life with a deafening roar and a rattle of vibrating metal.

"Gosh!" said Heath.

The children exchanged doubtful looks, but Goldenrod said briskly, "Okay—who's going to ride up front with me, and who wants to sit in the back?"

Laurel and Susan both wanted to ride in the cab, Laurel because she hated looking at scenery backwards, Susan because she said it was too dirty in the back. (Mostly what she wanted was to be *inside* somewhere, away from so much space.) Goldenrod said there wasn't room for them both up front, and that Laurel ought to have first choice.

Grumbling, Susan climbed into the back with the

others, pushing aside an ancient tarpaulin, an assortment of greasy tools, a much-patched spare tire, and a dented gas can.

"At least we won't run out of gas," Val observed, hefting the can. "It feels almost full."

"Maybe there aren't any gas stations out here," Susan said gloomily. She added, "Where do you think he is, anyway—the man who owns this truck? There's no place to go *to* that I can see."

Before anyone could answer, Goldenrod had put the truck in gear, and they were jolting off down the highway.

"Ow!" Susan braced her back more securely against the rear of the cab and sat staring up at the sky, since there wasn't anything else to look at. But now it didn't seem quite as lonely and empty as it had at first. Fat white clouds softened the harsh lines of the mountain peaks; and once she thought she saw a hawk circling high above—or could it be an eagle?

Val had spotted a windmill in the distance and was explaining to Heath how windmills could be used to pump water from the ground in a dry season. Meanwhile Daisy clung to the side of the truck, hoping to see something exciting, like a jackrabbit or a giant tumbleweed . . . or maybe a bunch of cattle rustlers galloping along, with a posse in full pursuit.

The highway ran straight as a ruler through the grasslands, but after a few miles it began to climb almost imperceptibly. They had a glimpse of a gleaming river over to their right, with clumps of what Laurel thought must be cottonwood trees. But still they'd seen no cattle or horses, no buildings, no sign of a ranch.

"Let's take the first turn we come to," Laurel yelled to Goldenrod over the rattle of the truck. "Look—isn't that a road up ahead?"

Goldenrod slowed down obediently but said, "This thing isn't going to climb any mountains, I hope you realize."

"Oh, these are just hills," Laurel said, as they made the turn onto a narrower, bumpier road with a gravelled surface. "The real mountains are still miles away."

"Hey!" There was a yell from the back as they hit a pothole with a clang and almost lost the tailgate. "Take it easy up there, will you?"

The road got rougher as the landscape changed about them. The open range still flowed away on one side; but on the other there were outcroppings of rock now, half-hidden in thickets of wild currant and gooseberry. Aspen trees fluttered their gold-and-crimson leaves against the sky, and small pines and junipers clung tough-rooted among the rocks.

Suddenly the mountains seemed to have moved much closer. Peering through the grimy windshield, Laurel could see fresh snow glittering on a rugged peak that seemed to tower almost overhead.

"I saw a porcupine!" Daisy exclaimed, as the truck jounced and groaned around a bend. "Well, I did," she insisted, though nobody had the breath to argue with her; they were all clinging to the sides of the truck now.

"Maybe we'll get to see some deer," Heath suggested. "Or antelope. Or a mountain lion, even."

"Not if they hear us coming first," Val said, somewhat grimly. A sliding wrench had just struck him smartly on the knee.

"Cows! I mean cattle!" Susan was pointing out over

72

the plains to a broad valley where a brown-and-white herd was drifting like a great patchwork cloud. "Laurel wants to see a ranch. Maybe—"

But she got no further. There was a violent jolt. The truck slewed sideways, spilling them together in a heap, and bumped painfully to a stop. It was pitched over at such an angle that they had trouble untangling their arms and legs.

Goldenrod switched off the engine and leaned out of the cab.

"Is everybody okay?" she said anxiously. "I'm afraid we've got a flat."

They all clambered down to inspect the damage. The left rear tire gave a last hiss of escaping air and collapsed It hadn't been much of a tire to begin with, they saw, covered with patches, the treads worn thin.

"Oh, gosh," Susan said in dismay. "And it isn't even our truck!"

They stood staring at it, while a magpie chattered derisively at them from the branch of a tree.

"Well, we've got a jack, anyway," Val said. "I should know, it kept banging into me."

"I don't know. . . ." Goldenrod was studying the position of the truck. Despite its age and dilapidation, it was a heavy vehicle.

"I can change a tire all right, but I'll need help. And the way it's leaning—well, I wouldn't want anyone to get hurt."

"But we can't just leave it here," Heath objected. "And anyway, what would we do then?"

"We could take a walk." Goldenrod looked up the road, which seemed to become steeper and rockier with every turn. "Or—well, I guess we could just go home."

73

There was a general outcry at this. Only Laurel remained silent. She kicked at a stone with the toe of her riding boot (she'd decided to wear her boots, just in case) and stared hard at a clump of purple asters beside the road, trying not to cry.

"Hey!" Daisy said suddenly. "Somebody's coming! Look—it's a cowboy!"

They all heard it then—a distant thunder of hoofbeats, just like on TV—and turned to look. A rider was galloping toward them across the plains. He called out something and waved his hat.

"A palomino," Laurel breathed, their predicament forgotten; she had eyes only for the horse. "Isn't he beautiful?"

"Listen, it's that cowboy that's beautiful," Goldenrod told her. "Especially if he knows something about cars and not just horses."

In a matter of minutes the rider had covered the distance. He set his horse at the gentle slope that joined the road just ahead, reined it around sharply, and jogged toward them: a tall young man with curly dark hair and sharp blue eyes, wearing chaps over his jeans, and a worn denim jacket.

"Saw you folks were having a problem," he greeted them, with a nod at the truck. Then his eyes narrowed; he stared hard from them to the truck and back again. But all he said was, "Hope there's a spare in the back of that thing."

He swung off his horse, dropping the reins over its head, and walked over to examine the spare tire Val was dragging out of the back of the pickup.

"Got air in it, at least," he observed. "And it ain't in

74

any worse shape than the one you've got on there. Okay, son, let's have that jack."

Susan, who couldn't help feeling responsible for the poor old truck—after all, the whole thing had been her idea in the first place—watched unhappily as they set about changing the tire. Maybe they could leave some money on the front seat to pay for fixing the flat, she thought. If it could be fixed; there hardly seemed room for another patch.

"What's your horse's name?" Laurel asked shyly.

"Him? That's Old Spurge," the cowboy answered without looking around. "Just a tired old buckskin pony, but he's real smart. Sometimes I think he knows the stock better'n I do."

Laurel bit her lip. Old Spurge hadn't looked so tired, galloping across the range . . . and a buckskin, not a palomino? Surely he was too big to be a pony. Cowpony, he must mean.

Daisy said curiously, "Won't he run away? You didn't tie him up or anything."

The cowboy laughed. "Oh, he's well-trained, miss. Reins over his head that way, he'll stand as long as he's supposed to. Old Spurge knows better than to run off on me."

At last the spare was on. The cowboy stood up, tossing the jack into the pickup, and wiped his hands on a rag. He said casually, turning to Goldenrod, "You folks staying around these parts for long?"

"Uh—well, no, not exactly." Goldenrod looked at her watch. "In fact, we'd better start heading back for the highway right now."

"Oh, now, I'd hate to see you do that, miss," the cowboy said.

His tone was amiable, but the children exchanged alarmed glances. Did he know the truck was stolen? Not that it was, exactly, but—

"Long as you've got this far," the cowboy was saying, "you ought to come on out to the ranch. Only another mile or so—and Ma gets lonely for company, now the guest season's over. She'd have my hide if I let you folks go off without even saying hello."

He swung himself lightly back into the saddle and grinned down at them in the friendliest possible way. "Besides, ain't no place to turn that contraption around till you get there."

Well, that was probably true enough. They thanked him and piled back into the truck, deciding there was nothing sinister about his invitation, after all. This was just that Western hospitality you were always hearing about.

Slowly the truck bumped off behind Old Spurge, gears whining. "Can't go much faster than a horse, anyway," Goldenrod said between her teeth. "Not on this road." She wrenched at the wheel, steering around rocks and potholes and washouts.

But Laurel wasn't listening. "Guest season." Did that mean it was only a dude ranch? she wondered, with a twinge of disappointment. Still, a dude ranch would be better than nothing. . . .

But the Lazy L turned out to be a kind of combination, as they found out later—a working ranch that also took in a few paying guests during the summer tourist season. The Lazy L! Laurel stared at the rough sign nailed to the gate. Maybe this was the L that had brought them here, and never mind Laramie.

"Oh!" she said, leaning forward in her seat. "Oh, Goldenrod, isn't it just *perfect?*"

The ranch lay in a narrow valley—a jumble of low buildings protected on the north and west by mountains and giving way on the east to the rolling plains of the open range. There was a stream shaded by cottonwoods, their heart-shaped leaves pale gold in the sunlight. A pond glittered like a chip of sky in the rough pasture beyond the ranchhouse. In the pure air, details stood out sharp and clear—a twist of chimney smoke, hollyhocks glowing against the white wall of the house, a water bucket slung over a fencepost, gleaming like old pewter.

"Nice," Goldenrod agreed. "I wonder if they've got any use for another truck."

The cowboy had ridden on ahead. As the truck bounced along the rough track between barns and corrals, they could see him talking to a plump woman on the front porch of the ranchouse. They seemed to be laughing about something.

The woman came forward, accompanied by a big black and white collie. "You can leave the truck there by the woodpile," she called to Goldenrod. "Any place will do." This seemed to strike her funny; she had to stop a moment to catch her breath before she came on to greet them, the collie capering ahead.

"I'm Emma Larkspur," she said, holding out her hand and smiling at them with eyes as blue as her son's. "Curt tells me you had some trouble with this old truck. Well, I'm glad it brought you here, anyhow. It's an ill wind that blows nobody good, I always say."

Curt, who had come up behind her, leading Old Spurge, gave a sudden guffaw at this remark. Goldenrod eyed him suspiciously.

Heath was patting the collie. "He sure is a nice dog," he said politely. "He didn't even bark at us."

"Well—" Curt began, his eyes still dancing; but his mother said briskly, "Well, children, I expect you'd like to see around the ranch, now you're here. And Curt, why don't you saddle up one of the horses for this young lady?" She nodded at Laurel's boots. "Looks like she came all ready to ride."

"Oh, I . . ." Laurel flushed with pleasure and embarrassment, wishing she hadn't bothered to polish her high Eastern riding boots that morning. Even if they were only secondhand, they looked kind of silly here.

"Maybe they'd *all* like a little ride," Curt drawled, with a significant glance at his mother. "Up along the rim trail, for instance. That's a nice easy ride and real pretty this time of year."

"What a good idea," Mrs. Larkspur agreed; and before anyone could say anything, Curt was herding them all toward one of the corrals. "Hey, Sam!" he called. "Help me saddle up, will you? Got some guests who want to ride."

An elderly cowhand appeared, and he and Curt began rapidly rounding up and saddling horses. When Val pointed out nervously that none of them even knew how to ride, except for Laurel, Curt assured him that these were all gentle trail horses, used to beginners. "All you have to do is sit on 'em. Right, Sam?"

"Right," Sam agreed. "Never lost a guest yet."

Even Goldenrod was persuaded to get up on a big raw-boned gray horse named Sassafras.

"I don't like the way he hangs his head," she said uneasily. "And those red eyes. . . . He isn't mean, is he?"

"Mean?" Sam wheezed with laughter. "Heck, he's just sleepy, miss. Old Sassafras here, he's sound asleep on the trail most of the time."

"What happens if he wakes up all of a sudden?" Goldenrod demanded.

Sam shook his head. "Doubt if you could tell the difference."

They filed out of the corral, with Curt in the lead on Old Spurge and Laurel bringing up the rear on the dainty little bay mare Curt had chosen for her. Her stirrups felt too long, but Curt said that was the way they were supposed to be. "Just stick out your feet and don't try to post when she trots. And when you want to turn her, don't pull on her mouth—just lay the reins against her neck, like so."

Curt was awfully nice, Laurel thought; and so good looking, too. Funny how Goldenrod didn't even seem to notice.

Their way led them up a rock trail beyond the ranch house. Most of the little valley was in shadow now, but as they climbed, they emerged into the sunshine once more. A light breeze twinkled the leaves of the aspens along the trail—"quakin' asp," Curt called them. The horses plodded along quietly, and after a while nobody worried too much about the steep drop on one side. Even Goldenrod began to relax, riding close behind Daisy's little calico pony. Sassafras was used to following the pony automatically, Sam had explained. "That way he don't even have to look up."

There was a hairpin turn, then a last sharp climb, and suddenly they found themselves in a high mountain meadow, green from melting snows and starred with late wildflowers. They reined up in silence, struck dumb by the magnificence of the view—the golden plains, the mountains, the tiny buildings of the ranch far below, with the stream twisting through them like a length of bright wire.

"First blizzard'll be along pretty soon, though," Curt observed, glancing at the high peaks to the west, sharp-cut against the brilliant sky.

"But it's not even winter yet," Heath protested.

Curt laughed. "Tell that to the mountains."

While he was describing the rigors of a Wyoming winter to the boys, Susan whispered to Goldenrod, "What are we going to do about the truck? We'll never get it back to where we found it in time."

"I know." Goldenrod leaned back in her saddle, stretching her legs. Already she looked at ease on a horse, as though she'd been riding all her life. Even Sassafras looked different somehow, his head up and his ears pricked back as she spoke. "I don't think we'd ever make it back over that road, anyway, not without another flat tire. So . . ." She shrugged. "Let's just hope the owner has some insurance. That truck's worth more lost than found, that's for sure."

Curt said he'd take them back down to the ranch by another trail, after a trot across the meadow. "No fair hanging onto the saddle horn," he called, as they bounced along, but only Laurel and Goldenrod managed without it. Susan felt as if her saddle had turned to cement; it was a relief when they slowed to a walk and began heading down again.

"This next stretch is pretty steep," Curt told them. "Just sit back and keep your reins loose."

They were filing down into a narrow gorge walled on either side by sheer slabs of rock. The horses' hooves rang out sharply in this enclosed place, and the air was suddenly chill without the warmth of the sun. Spooky—they all felt it, and some of their earlier mistrust of Curt returned. Remembering TV westerns, they couldn't help thinking how loud a gunshot would sound in a place like this. A perfect spot for an ambush, too, right there at that bend in the trail. . . .

Which was nonsense, of course; but they were all glad when the trail leveled off at last in a mossy glen lined with ferns, and there was soft earth under their horses' feet again. One more wide sweep of the trail, and they were back almost where they'd started, at the gates of the Lazy L. A few lights shone now in the windows of the ranch house and bunkhouse, and the stream ran placidly along beneath the rustling leaves of the cotton-woods. There was the woodpile, and the big water trough, with the blue truck parked beside it, and—

And a red-faced man in a sheepskin jacket who was standing beside the truck, shaking his fist and yelling furiously as they approached.

"You—Curt! What do you think you're doing with my truck?"

The children froze in their saddles, and Goldenrod said, "Oh-oh."

But Curt's shoulders were shaking with laughter. He reined up and said over his shoulder, "Now, don't worry, I'll handle this. Maybe you shouldn't have taken it, but it serves him right. Old Harvey Knapweed and his precious truck!" He shook his head, still laughing. "Wait'll this one gets around."

"Is he a friend of yours?" Heath asked uncertainly.

81

"Well, maybe not right at this minute. A neighbor, anyhow—owns of the biggest ranches around. Drives a Cadillac when he's in town, but the rest of the time he rattles around in that old heap of his. First truck he ever owned—says it brings him luck."

"Sort of like a horseshoe?" Daisy said.

"Sort of." Curt grinned. "Not that we're exactly short of horseshoes around here. . . . Anyhow," he went on, "old Harvey won't spend a nickel on that truck, not even for new tires; but he won't part with it, either. Only trouble is, it won't take him anywhere he wants to go without breaking down. His foreman has to follow him around in the jeep, and if Harvey wants to go out on the range or somewhere, why he just leaves the truck wherever he happens to be. Says that's part of the good luck—nobody'd ever steal the thing. And then you kids come along . . ." Curt threw back his head again.

"He looks pretty mad," Val said uneasily, as they started forward once more.

Mrs. Larkspur had come out of the house and seemed to be trying to soothe Mr. Knapweed, who kept shaking his head angrily.

"Oh, Harvey ain't such a bad guy. It'll strike him funny, too, once he gets over being surprised."

Goldenrod said thoughtfully, "So that's why you wanted to keep us here—you and your mother. What did she do, phone him while we were out riding?"

Curt nodded. "We didn't want you hightailing it out of here in that rattletrap and losing it somewhere. There'd be no living with Harvey then. Besides, you might have had real trouble with it—steering wheel coming right off in your hands, something like that." He flashed them all a grin. "You had a pretty good ride, though, didn't you? Maybe you'll feel a little stiff in the morning, but nothing to what that truck could do to you."

Laurel saw Goldenrod glance nervously at her watch. It occurred to her that they were going to have some awkward questions to answer in the next few minutes. Like where they'd come from, how they'd happened to find the truck in the first place, how they were planning to get home from here. As for paying Mr. Knapweed for the flat tire—well, Laurel thought, it looked as if he might need a whole new set of tires just to get back out to the highway.

This struck her funny; she was about to say something to Goldenrod, when a chipmunk darted out from under the woodpile and ran right under her horse's feet. The mare shied violently, reared, and then shot forward, leaving Laurel behind. She sailed through the air and landed with a tremendous splash in the water trough.

"Hey, there!" Mr. Knapweed broke off his harangue and came hurrying over. "You all right, gal?"

Laurel sat up, spluttering, and managed to nod. She wondered if she'd ruined her riding boots, and hoped she had. She'd much rather have a pair of beat-up old cowboy boots like Curt's. This thought made her giggle, and she swallowed a mouthful of water. Mr. Knapweed was holding out his hand gallantly to her, but she was laughing too hard to take it.

"Laurel!" Goldenrod was clambering off her horse— on the wrong side, Laurel saw, which made her laugh even harder. "Listen, we're going home right now. Stay there!" she added—as if Laurel had made any move to get out.

Ignoring the stares of Curt and his mother and Mr.

Knapweed, Goldenrod sat down cross-legged on the muddy ground beside the water trough, crossed her arms, and closed her eyes. "Everybody get their feet out of the stirrups," she ordered. "We don't want to take the horses, too. Laurel, stop laughing! We've got to concentrate."

So Laurel did; though she thought this might really be the end of the living room rug.

Chapter **8** *Goldenrod at Work*

"Oh, dear," Mrs. Madder said distractedly one Saturday morning, peering into the refrigerator. "We seem to be out of everything at once. I suppose it's time I did a real marketing." She sighed. "And Val needs a new parka, and Daisy's already outgrown her school shoes—"

Val's face darkened at the prospect of being dragged shopping on a Saturday morning, and his mother didn't look much happier. Mrs. Madder hated shopping at any time, but especially when she was beginning a new picture.

Horses, she thought. Why horses, for heaven's sake, when she hadn't even sketched a horse in years? But that was what she saw—the shapes of horses, plodding up across her canvas at a sharp diagonal, as if climbing a steep hill. Except that in one corner there was a different kind of shape entirely, something oblong and blue. An interesting *rusty* shade of blue, if there was such a color—

Daisy said, "If we're going marketing, can we go to Goldenrod's store? We never get to see her when she's working."

"She probably isn't there on Saturdays," Mrs. Madder replied absently. She was still puzzling over the blue oblong.

"Yes, she is," Susan said, coming into the kitchen to sharpen a pencil. "She has her day off on Tuesdays."

"Please, Mother!" Daisy begged.

"It's not that far," Val contributed, cheering up a little at the prospect of seeing Goldenrod. "The supermarket, I mean. It's in that new shopping center on the way to Verner Falls."

"What?" With an effort, Mrs. Madder wrenched her mind away from the painting. "Oh. Well, I suppose we could. There's a shoe store there, I think, and an Army-Navy store—you might find a parka there, Val. And everybody needs new jeans—"

"Oh, good," said Daisy. "Let's all go and surprise Goldenrod!"

Her mother said, "Goldenrod probably sees enough of you during the week, as it is. And if you have homework to do, Susan . . ." She looked at the pencil in Susan's hand.

"Oh, I was just making a list," Susan said airily. "I can finish it later."

"Well. . . ." Mrs. Madder hesitated, and then gave in. "All right. Find Laurel and Heath and tell them we're leaving right away. I'd like to be back by lunchtime."

Val and Susan exchanged grins. Whenever their mother took them shopping, there always seemed to be a dozen extra errands she might as well do along the way. At some point she would discover in surprise that it was long past lunchtime, and wind up treating them all at a Friendly's or McDonald's.

As they started off in the car, Mrs. Madder remarked, "You know, this isn't such a bad idea. I have the oddest feeling about that girl sometimes. As if she weren't quite real, and might just—well, *disappear* someday, when you weren't looking."

The children stirred uneasily, and their mother added quickly, "Oh, I'm not trying to check up on her. If Goldenrod says she works at the supermarket, I'm sure she does. It's just that there's something so—vague about her. I've never heard her mention her friends or family, or a boyfriend; or even where she lives. Have you?"

They shook their heads.

"Of course everyone's entitled to their privacy," Mrs. Madder went on; indeed, this was something she believed in strongly. "But with Goldenrod—well, somehow you don't even dare ask questions. As if she might just bolt, like a startled deer."

She smiled at her own fancy, but nobody said anything. They knew exactly what their mother meant; and also how easy it would be for Goldenrod to "bolt" if she wanted to. In fact, as they approached the supermarket, they began to wonder unhappily if Goldenrod would be there after all. Maybe she *wasn't* quite real, as their mother said. Or could it be, Laurel thought, that her baby-sitting afternoons were just "trips" from some other, unimaginable place?

87

But the first person they saw as they entered the store was Goldenrod, wearing a yellow smock that almost matched her hair. She was at the Quick-Check counter— "12 Items or Less"—flicking away with practiced speed at the cash register, handing out change, sliding things into paper bags, then turning with a smile to the next customer. She did everything so fast, it was like watching a sleight-of-hand act.

"Goldenrod!" Heath called, as Mrs. Madder went off in search of an empty cart. She looked up and saw them, smiled, nodded over at one of the regular counters to show she'd move when they were ready to be checked out, and went on ringing up a sale—all without missing a beat.

"Wow!" said Val, grinning; but his tone expressed the secret relief they all felt. They hurried off after their mother, to tease her into buying all the things she never bought unless they were with her—frozen pies and cupcakes, marshmallows, doughnuts, popcorn.

"The dentist bills will come out of your allowances," Mrs. Madder said grimly as Susan added a box of coconut-flavored cereal to the loaded cart. "Ugh, it's pink! How on earth can anyone eat *pink* cereal?" Never mind the fact that she herself was apt to paint trees orange and oranges green; cereal ought to be cereal-colored, Mrs. Madder felt.

While she was wandering up and down the dairy aisle trying to find the Swiss cheese, two girls wearing yellow smocks like Goldenrod's came out of a door marked "Employees Only" and stood talking a moment before going on to their posts. Laurel and Val, who were nearby, couldn't help overhearing their conversation.

"Okay, so she's fast," one of the girls said. "I give her

that. But *friendly*? Listen, have you ever heard her say anything except 'hello,' 'thank you,' and 'goodbye?' "

"Well, the customers like her," the other girl said with a shrug. "That's what the award's supposed to be for."

"And I suppose that gives her the right to look through the rest of us like we're not even there? After all, we're the ones who have to work with her." An indignant snort. "Who does she think she is, anyway, I'd like to know? And *Goldenrod*—what a name!"

"Maybe she's just shy," the second girl ventured. "I mean, she's still pretty new here."

"Shy!" The first girl gave a snort. "Listen, you know Sam in the meat department, that half the girls here would give their right arms to date? Well, he asked *her* to go out with him—and you know what she said? 'Sorry, but I don't date.' Just like that. Shy! Snotty is more like it, if you ask me."

"Still," the other girl said uncertainly, "maybe if we tried to get to know her better—"

"*You* can try." The first girl turned away. "I give up."

Laurel and Val looked at each other, dismayed by what they'd heard.

"Well," Val said, after a moment, "I guess Goldenrod won some kind of award, anyway."

"Yes." Laurel frowned. "But gosh—if nobody likes her . . . You'd think she'd *want* to make friends."

"Well, she's not like that with us," Val said staunchly. "Unfriendly, or stuck-up, or—well, the way they said."

But when they joined the line at the checkout counter, they saw what the girls meant. Goldenrod was packing a large order, five or six bags' worth of groceries. At the same time she was answering questions about prices from an inexperienced clerk at the next counter, and opening new rolls of change. Yet when one of the other girls—the one who'd spoken up for her—came over to help, Goldenrod shook her head.

"I can manage, thanks," she said. Her voice was pleasant enough, but cool. The girl stood looking at her for a moment and then turned away with a shrug.

Even when the Madders' turn came, Goldenrod's manner remained brisk and impersonal—as though they were no more than distant acquaintances, Laurel thought. Only when all the bags were packed and they were ready to go did she seem for a moment like the Goldenrod they knew.

"There," she said, handing Daisy the last bag. "You sure that isn't too heavy for you, Daisy?"

"Oh, no," Daisy said. She was gazing admiringly at Goldenrod's yellow smock, which had "Goldenrod" written in curly white letters across the pocket. "I'm going to have a job like this when I grow up," she announced. "Only I have to go get better at arithmetic first," she added, eyeing the big cash register with respect.

Goldenrod and Mrs. Madder exchanged smiles; there was a tinge of sadness in Goldenrod's. "Oh, there'll be lots of other jobs you can do when you grow up, Daisy," she said. "You might change your mind before then."

"But *you* decided to do it," Daisy said, "and you like it, you said you did."

"Well, yes. But—"

There were more customers waiting in line. Goldenrod turned to them with a bright, apologetic smile, and said hastily over her shoulder, "See you on Monday, kids." Tap-tap-tap-tap-*zing* went the cash register.

"What's wrong with being a checkout girl?" Daisy demanded of Laurel as they crossed the parking lot to the car.

"Nothing's *wrong* with it, Daisy. It just might get to be sort of boring after a while. And—well, it's not the kind of job you'd want to do all your life."

"I wouldn't, anyway," Daisy said promptly. "I'm going to get married and have two children, a girl and a boy. And my husband is always going to stay home and take care of us."

This was the kind of remark Laurel never quite knew how to deal with. She looked at Daisy's small face—stubborn and yet somehow anxious, too—and then at her mother. Mrs. Madder didn't seem to have heard. She was studying her shopping list with a frown and glancing at her watch.

"Oh, dear," she said. "It's going to be awfully late by the time we get home. I suppose we'd better have lunch here, if there's any place—"

"Hey, there's a Friendly's right over there!" Heath said, with an air of discovery. (They had all spotted it the moment they drove in.)

"Is there? Well, all right," said Mrs. Madder. She added sternly, "But absolutely *no* banana splits or fancy desserts today—not after all the junk you've already made me buy."

They managed not to smile. It was Mrs. Madder who loved banana splits and always wound up having one. It was a perfectly simple thing to make at home, she would say with a puzzled air, if you wanted to go to all the trouble. So why did they always taste so much better when you were out somewhere?

Susan too was thinking about bananas, but for a different reason. Bananas and cocoanuts and palm trees and white sand beaches . . .

Susan's trip was next, and she had been planning it for days. In her methodical way, she had drawn up a long list of places beginning with S, arranged in alphabetical order. It included Shaker Heights, Ohio (her second grade teacher had moved there), Spain, Staten Island (because of the ferry), Sweden, Switzerland, and Sydney, Australia.

She had almost decided on Switzerland when she discovered the Caribbean. All those S islands named after saints—St. Vincent, St. Thomas, St. Lucia, St. Croix. . . . With the weather at home turning cold and raw, Susan thought a nice sunny island might be just the thing. But which one to choose?

She announced her decision a few days later.

"St. Martin?" Val said suspiciously. "Where's that?"

Heath looked crushed. He had been hoping against hope that Susan would choose the Sahara Desert. Susan told him she didn't *want* to go to a desert, and if Heath did, he'd just have to wait his turn. He said sadly that he didn't think there were any deserts beginning with H— not big ones, anyway.

Susan said, "Well, at least there's plenty of sand where we're going, Heath—only it's beaches, not deserts. St. Martin's an island," she explained. "People go there for vacations. Part of it belongs to France and part of it belongs to Holland, and—well, look, this is where I read about it."

She produced an old travel section from a Sunday newspaper. Their mother had a huge stack of newspapers up in the attic, which she had been meaning for years to give to some paper drive. But the pile had grown so big now that it would take a truck to move it; so there the papers stayed, and it was there that Susan had come across the article on St. Martin.

They pored over it, studying the pictures. In one of them people were sunbathing on a great stretch of dazzling white sand. "Oh, boy, we can take our bathing suits!" Daisy said happily. Another picture showed a street scene—immaculate little houses with brightly painted shutters and picket fences and neat gardens of exotic-looking flowers.

"That's the Dutch side," Susan said importantly, looking over their shoulders.

In fact, this was one of the reasons she'd chosen St. Martin. Susan longed to go to Holland, where everything sounded so neat and tidy and clean; but she knew Heath would never choose Holland. It wouldn't be adventurous enough for him.

"It sounds crazy," Val said. "How can a place belong to two different countries at once?"

"It tells about it here." Susan found the paragraph she wanted and read it aloud. " 'According to legend, landing parties from a French and a Dutch ship arrived on the island at the same time. Instead of fighting over it, they decided that the leaders of each party would begin walking around the island in opposite directions. Where they met, a line would be drawn back to the starting point, thus dividing the island fairly between the two nations.' "

Laurel looked at the small map on the opposite page. "It doesn't look too fair. The French got more of it."

" 'The Frenchman covered more ground,' " Susan read, " 'but the shrewd Dutchman claimed for his country the more valuable part of the island, including a

93

large and profitable salt pond just behind the present Dutch capital of Philipsburg."

"You mean they never even had a war?" Val sounded disappointed.

"I guess not. It says the two countries have shared the island peacefully ever since. There isn't even a real border, just a sign that tells you when you're going from one side to the other."

Heath was frowning at the bright pictures. "I hope there won't be too many people there," he said. "You know—tourists."

"Oh, it's just a little island," Susan assured him. "They only have a few hotels and some shops. 'Simple and unspoiled,'" she read from the article.

Laurel looked at the date of the paper. "It could have changed, though," she said. "I mean, this was written quite a while ago."

Susan shrugged impatiently. "Well, even if there are a few more people and shops and things, it still won't be *crowded*. Now," she said busily, picking up one of her lists. "First of all we'll go to Philipsburg. Then we'll go look at the salt pond. After that we can take a bus over to the French side—the main town there's called Marigot —and then—"

The others sighed. Once Susan started planning, they knew, there was no way of stopping her. By the time they left, she'd probably have their whole tour of the island charted out, down to the very last minute. On the other hand, with only a few hours to spend there, maybe that wasn't such a bad thing.

Chapter 9 Susan's Trip

"Are you sure you have all the details right?" Susan asked Goldenrod anxiously. "Like—well, it isn't a *jungly* kind of island, for instance." No chance of crocodiles, she meant.

Goldenrod shrugged. She had dressed for the trip in a blue sundress, white sandals, and white shell earrings and was beginning to look cold, sitting on the Madders' old green couch. Outside a winter storm was raging, blowing sleet against the windowpanes and howling around the corners of the house.

"I read the same article you did," she said. "I don't see what there is to get wrong. I did all right in Wyoming, didn't I?"

"Except for the truck," Val reminded her. He added with a grin, "I wonder what they thought when we all just disappeared like that—Curt and his mother and Mr. Knapweed."

"And the horses," Heath said. "Gosh, I wonder what *they* thought."

The more they considered this, the funnier it got—that and the picture of Laurel sailing into the water trough.

"Come on!" Susan said crossly. "How can I concentrate when everybody's laughing? Now you've got Goldenrod laughing, too. And Laurel, are you really going to wear that *hat?*"

Laurel said with dignity, "Listen, the sun down there is a lot hotter than we're used to. It's only sensible to wear a hat." The hat in question was one their mother sometimes wore for gardening—a battered straw with a wide frayed brim.

"Well, it looks peculiar," Susan said.

Indeed, they all looked and felt rather peculiar, sitting around in their lightest summer shorts and shirts, their arms and legs winter-pale. On their laps they held their bathing suits in rolled-up towels. Outside the sleet was turning to snow.

Goldenrod put on an enormous pair of sunglasses, picked up the beach bag that contained the sunburn cream and extra towels and Val's mask and snorkel, and said, "Okay, let's go. I'm getting goose bumps."

She settled into position, gave a nod to Susan—who had already gone rigid with concentration—and added with a sigh, "Oh, boy, is that sun going to feel good!"

There was the familiar drowsiness, the sense of floating, drifting, sliding . . . only this time it wasn't like a water slide, it was more like going over a waterfall. Or like standing under one—under an enormous warm shower that drenched you in an instant, sluicing down in great blinding sheets.

It took them all a few moments to realize that they had arrived in St. Martin in the midst of a tropical downpour—they and what seemed like several thousand other people, all of them hurrying for shelter along the narrow sidewalks of Philipsburg.

"Help!" cried Daisy, dodging a party of large women in plastic raincoats who were bent on squeezing themselves into an already crowded jewelry store.

"Let's get out of this," Laurel agreed in a panicky voice. The crowd had jostled her off the curb, almost into the path of a large American car.

They were all soaked to the skin by the time they found refuge on the deserted town dock, beneath a corrugated tin roof on which the rain drummed noisily.

"Who were all those *people?*" Heath asked breathlessly.

But nobody knew.

"Look," said Susan, bravely trying to make the best of things. "There's the Dutch flag and the French flag, too. So this must be St. Martin, all right." She pointed at a building across the square opposite them.

The wind blew the curtain of rain aside for a moment, and they were able to make out the colors of the two flags, flapping wetly from their poles. This might be sunny St. Martin; but they couldn't help thinking they would have been a lot drier just staying at home.

"And to think I was worrying about the sun!" Laurel said mournfully. The crown of her hat was plastered to her head; the brim hung almost to her shoulders in great soggy pleats.

With which the rain stopped, exactly as if someone had turned off a tap, and the sun came out.

"It's like a curtain going up!" Susan exclaimed in delight.

Like a giant spotlight, the sunshine threw the scene before them into brilliant relief. The red roofs of Philipsburg glistened against a backdrop of abrupt green hills. In the waters of the bay, rough fishing boats bobbed side by side with sleek sailboats and motor yachts. The water itself deepened in color as they looked, almost as if someone were pouring blue dye into it.

And then, like an apology for the storm, a perfect rainbow appeared—a great shimmering arc that seemed to spring from the highest of the green peaks all the way to the water's edge, burying itself in the golden sand only a hundred yards from where they stood.

"My gosh!" said Heath.

But he wasn't looking at the rainbow. He was gazing in dismay at the square. There were all those people again—and not just people, *tourists*. All the women seemed to be carrying large shopping bags, and the men were festooned with cameras. There was a dazed, hectic look on their sunburned faces, as if they weren't quite sure where they were or what was supposed to happen next.

" 'Simple and unspoiled'?" Laurel quoted, looking at the bumper-to-bumper traffic on Front Street.

Susan said uncertainly, "I guess they must have built some more hotels, or something."

But Val said, "Hey! I bet that's a cruise boat out there." He was pointing to a huge white ship anchored far out in the bay. "That must be where they're all coming from."

Some of the tourists were strolling out toward the dock now. One man took a picture of Goldenrod and the children, as if they were an official part of the scenery. "Maybe it's my wet hat," Laurel said with a giggle. "An old island custom." As a matter of fact, the hat felt quite comfortable now under the fierce rays of the Caribbean sun.

Nearby, a small brown island boy had been tapping out an infectious rhythm with his hands on one of the big oil drums beside the dock. Now he looked around with a smile and said, "Big ship, she come in this morning. Two more coming tomorrow. It is a lively time," he added, which seemed something of an understatement.

"Well, I'm glad we didn't come tomorrow, anyway," Heath grumbled.

"Is the whole island like this?" Goldenrod asked. The boy looked puzzled. "Crowded, I mean."

He shrugged. "Rich Americans, they like the shops, maybe they visit the big hotels, swim in the pools. But elsewhere . . ." He considered. "It is more peaceful by the French side, perhaps."

"Then let's go there," urged Laurel, who was hoping for a chance to try out her French, irregular verbs and all. Most of the people here spoke English, she knew— a lilting, different kind of English, judging by this boy's speech—but still. . . .

"I want to see the salt pond first," said Susan, stubbornly clinging to her original plan of action. "It's just behind the town, isn't it? So it can't be very far."

"Not far," the boy agreed; and added, "You will not be staying there long." It was more of a statement than a question.

"Well—no, I guess not," Susan said. "We want to see

99

as much of St. Martin as we can, and we don't have too much time."

"*And* we want to go swimming," Daisy reminded her. "In the sea."

The boy studied them curiously for a moment. Then he gave them his flashing smile, said, "I will speak to my Uncle Christophe now," and darted off across the square.

They looked at each other uncertainly; but a in a few minutes the boy returned, accompanied by a large, dignified-looking black man dressed in an immaculate white shirt and dark pants. His hair was grizzled, and his smile revealed a dazzle of gold teeth.

"I understand you people are wishing to see something of the island," he greeted them, in a courteous bass voice. "I, Christophe, am happy to oblige you. Plenty of room for all," he added, with an expansive gesture at a car parked in front of a nearby bait-and-tackle shop. It was a large green sedan, old but lovingly polished.

"Well . . ." Susan considered, while the others waited. It was Susan's trip, after all. Then she nodded. "Yes, that would be very nice, Christophe," she said, in an equally dignified manner. "It will save us a lot of time." Which turned out to be another understatement, though they didn't know it then.

They introduced themselves, and Christophe shook hands formally with each in turn. Then he ushered them over to the car, seating Susan and Goldenrod in front, the others in back.

"We'd like to see the salt pond first, please," Susan said importantly, as Christophe nosed the car into the stream of traffic along Front Street.

"Ah, yes." Christophe leaned out the window to wave

to a friend, at the same time spinning the wheel to avoid a car pulling out of a parking place. "We shall be passing the salt pond on our way out of town," he assured them, with a sudden blast of his horn at a party of tourists trying to cross the street. They jumped back just in time; Goldenrod winced.

The geography of Philipsburg was simple enough, they discovered. First came Front Street; then Back Street; and then a newer, broader street that Christophe said people just called the Other Street. It was this last that ran alongside the salt pond—a great square of gray-blue water, wrinkled by the trade wind, and surrounded by what appeared to be a blinding white sand beach.

"Not sand," Christophe explained, picking up speed. "Salt."

"Gosh," said Val, staring. "They must have had a real mining operation here once. I wonder how it worked."

He wished they could stop, or at least slow down to get a better look; but Christophe showed no sign of slackening speed, and Susan didn't ask him to. Because what was that *smell*, blowing into the car so strongly on the breeze? Maybe it was the dump—Susan looked with distaste at a pile of refuse where goats were browsing contentedly—but she had a feeling it might be the salt pond, too. No wonder Christophe's nephew had said they wouldn't be staying here long.

They seemed to be approaching a main road. At least there was a row of palms down the middle and a decorative little bridge.

"*Prinz Bernhard Bruge.*" Laurel read the sign as they approached. "*Bruge* must mean bridge," she said, pleased at having found a foreign word, even if it was Dutch.

"And now we are on the way to Marigot," Christophe announced comfortably, whipping around a curve and scattering chickens right and left.

Susan had been worrying about something. Now she cleared her throat and asked, "Are you—I mean, is this a taxi, Christophe?" It had occurred to her belatedly that this might turn out to be an expensive ride.

Christophe chuckled, shaking his head. "For twenty years I am a taxi driver," he explained. "But now—" He shrugged. "Too many cars, too much traffic on the island. It is extremely wearing for the nerves, you understand?"

They were tearing along a straight stretch now, toward a dead-end crossroads. It was hard to see much wrong with Christophe's nerves.

"So," he went on, swinging left at the crossroads with a squeal of brakes, "I am retired now, and living a quiet life. Occasionally"—he passed a motor bike, a man riding a donkey, and a large fuel truck—"I take passengers for my own pleasure. My nephew has told me you are in a hurry to see the island, and it is a lovely day for a drive, so . . ." He shrugged again and added graciously, "You will be my guests."

"Well, that's very nice of you—" Susan began; but was interrupted by a kind of yelp from Goldenrod.

"Hey! We're not in *that* much of a hurry," she protested, as they shot around a curve and began hurtling up the side of a very long steep hill.

"There will not be time to see all the beautiful places," Christophe continued regretfully. "However"—he took one hand from the wheel, and Goldenrod clenched her teeth—"you will have a fine view here from the top of the mountain."

If we get to the top alive, they couldn't help thinking. They turned their heads to look back at the way they had come. Now they could see the whole of Philipsburg strung out along its natural causeway, with the salt pond on one side and the glittering blue of the great bay on the other.

Christophe started to pass another car on a hairpin turn, thought better of it, and continued his travelogue. "After Marigot, we shall proceed to Grande Case"—he pronounced it *cause*—"where you may wish to stop for refreshments. Then I think you will enjoy to see Orient Bay, very beautiful, and after that—"

Susan was beginning to smoulder. Christophe might be a very nice man, but who was in charge of this trip, anyway? She was trying to think of a polite way to interrupt when they arrived at the top of the mountain. Christophe pulled over to the side of the road, with a sweeping gesture at the view before them.

"Wow!"

Even Goldenrod was impressed enough to unclench her teeth. Far below them lay a great inland lagoon, set like a jewel among low green hills and the shining white beaches of the outer shoreline. But it was the expanse of the sea itself that made them gasp, a deep cobalt blue in the afternoon sunlight. Islands floated mistily on the horizon. They listened raptly as Christophe named them off: Saba, St. Eustacius, St. Christopher, St. Barthélemy. . . .

"Yes, indeed," Christophe finished with a nod of satisfaction. "A beautiful sight. And now we had best be continuing on our journey."

He released the brake, spun the wheel, and shot back onto the road, almost into the path of one of the island buses. It hooted cheerfully at him and sailed by on a wave of laughter, brown arms waving through the open windows.

"That Percy," Christophe said, shaking his head and chuckling. "He is one crazy driver, mon."

They tore down the other side of the mountain. After a few zigzags, the road flattened and ran straight. They whipped along between rough fields where cattle grazed, past gaunt flamboyant trees, which in spring, Christophe said, would be a mass of fiery red blossoms. The frontier sign came and went in a blur of letters. *"Partie Francaise,"* Laurel read hastily. *"Bienvenue.* That means 'welcome,' I think. Hey—we're in France!"

"Well, I can't see any difference," Val complained. Even with all the windows open, it was warm and rather cramped in the back seat. "It all looks like a bunch of scenery to me."

Yet as they came to the outskirts of Marigot, even Val sat up and took notice. Here there was none of the Dutch tidiness of Philipsburg. Gas stations, tiny shacks, modern shops, cafés, whitewashed cottages bright with hibiscus and poinsettias, yards where goats and pigs and babies all tumbled about in the dust together. . . .

It was a bewildering mixture of old and new. As the traffic thickened, smart sports cars kept pace with women carrying their burdens in the traditional way—on the tops of their heads. Daisy stared in awe at one elderly woman who was balancing a whole case of soda bottles in this way.

But they saw little enough of Marigot itself. Christophe declared there were too many tourists today, and no place to park. They had a glimpse of a pastel-colored main street and the azure water of the harbor at its far end. "I never *believed* in that color!" Goldenrod marveled. "I always thought it was just for postcards." But already they were speeding onward to Grande Case.

"Wherever *that* is!" Susan grumbled under her breath. She was beginning to feel more like Christophe's prisoner than his guest. But there was no time to brood, not with so much to look at. The road was narrower and rougher now, and Christophe drove a little more cautiously—even using the brake on some of the worst curves. At the highest point of their journey, where the road made an impossible right-angled turn on the very edge of a cliff, he lifted a casual hand from the wheel and said, "Grande Case." Goldenrod had her eyes shut; but the others caught a dizzy glimpse of some red roofs and palms along the shore far below.

Soon they were plunging down to sea level again, through lusher country than they had yet seen. There were ferns and bamboo, wild bougainvillaea, banana trees, mangos, papaya, breadfruit. . . . Christophe pointed them out as they hurtled along, while Goldenrod looked ready to grab the wheel at any moment.

But at last they were running along the straight stretch of road that led to Grande Case—a village only one street wide, lined with small neat houses half-smothered in flowers. On their left shone the glassy turquoise blue of the sea.

The villagers waved and called greetings as they passed; everyone seemed to know Christophe. Just as they seemed to be leaving Grande Case behind without stopping after all (Susan had her mouth open to protest), he eased the car over to the curb, gave them his benevolent gold-toothed smile, and announced: "Now we shall all enjoy a cooling drink."

He led them to a café across the street, where he insisted on treating everyone to Cokes and potato chips. It seemed an odd kind of snack to be having in France, Laurel thought dazedly—or in a French village, anyway. She listened hard to the conversations around her. Some of them seemed to be in French, some in English, and some in a kind of mixture that she couldn't understand at all. She said *"Merci"* to the smiling island girl who served her Coke, but then couldn't think of anything else to say.

The others had taken their Cokes outside to gaze at the long dazzling sweep of the beach. Some boys were fishing from the town dock; an island schooner with much-patched sails was moored nearby. Just beyond, a group of pelicans floated on the swell, looking ridiculously solemn and beady-eyed, their long beaks tucked down coyly on their plump white breasts. Suddenly one rose into the air, hovered a moment, plunged like an arrow into the water, and came up with a wriggling silver fish.

"Oh!" said Daisy, clapping her hands. "Oh, I want to go swimming! Can't we go swimming here?"

Christophe had come to stand in the doorway behind them, beaming. "Very fine swimming here in Grande Case," he assured them. "Not crowded, you see." And indeed, except for the pelicans, there was no one at all in the turquoise water.

They changed into their suits in the rest rooms of the café, and raced back outside over the hot sand to fling themselves into the sea.

"Wow!" said Laurel.

"Gosh!" said Heath.

"I can see my toenails!" said Susan.

It was like no water they had ever swum in before—
neither warm nor cold, and as soft as silk on their skins.
They could see the tiny silver bubbles rising about their
ankles and the delicate colors of the small shells lying
on the wrinkled white sand at their feet. As for the color
of the water—as Heath said, raising a dripping arm to
examine it, you almost expected it to come *off* on you.

A kind of water-madness possessed them, each in his
own way. Val put on his mask and snorkel and cruised
about on the surface of the water, gazing entranced at
the fish flickering by unafraid in the transparent depths
beneath him. Closer to shore, Daisy did flips and rolls
and dives like an inspired porpoise. Susan decided to
practice every single stroke she'd learned at the Y last
year. How easy they all seemed, here in this buoyant
water! She never even ran out of breath.

"Hey! I can do the inverted breastroke!" she exclaimed.

But there was no one nearby to hear her. Heath had
swum far down the beach and was walking slowly back,
breathing in the great calm of sea and space. Laurel and
Goldenrod were floating lazily on their backs, letting the
water nudge them this way and that—gazing now at the
sky, now at the horizon, now at the long palm-fringed
curve of the beach. They could smell cooking fires and
hear a rooster crowing. A line of wash strung between
two almond trees stirred gently in the soft breeze.

"What are we going to do about Christophe?" Laurel
asked, after a while.

"How do you mean?" Goldenrod seemed almost
asleep, her hair floating mermaid-fashion on the swell.
She had said she wasn't much of a swimmer; but she
looked now as if she'd spent all of her life in the water.

"Well, he's been so nice to us. So how can we just—you know—just disappear?"

They'd left Christophe having a beer with the proprietor of the café and some cronies. "He may not even notice," Goldenrod said languidly.

"But there were all those other places he was going to take us to."

Goldenrod sat up in the water, yawning and blinking her green eyes. She looked more like a mermaid than ever. But she said practically, "Listen, the *worst* thing we could do is disappear while we're in the car. The way Christophe drives, that could be the end of him."

Laurel had to admit that was probably true. But there must be some way to explain, she thought. They couldn't just go off rudely, without even thanking Christophe, not after all his kindness to them. . . .

She was mulling this over—rather lazily, her eyes shut—when Goldenrod said sharply: "Hey—what's Daisy doing all the way out there? Daisy!" she called.

Laurel lifted her head, blinking, and saw that Daisy had swum out to join Val. At the moment they were both hovering motionless in the water, apparently looking at something just under the surface ahead of them.

"Oh, Daisy's a good swimmer," Laurel said confidently. "And Val will look after her—"

She stopped. There was something odd about the scene, she realized. Daisy had turned her head quickly at Goldenrod's call, but then had frozen again . . . almost as if, Laurel thought, she were afraid to move.

"Daisy!" she yelled. "Val! Are you okay?"

For a moment there was no response. Then Val called out something in a low hoarse voice. It took them both a horrified instant to realize what he had said.

"Barracuda!"

Goldenrod went into action. As she said afterwards, she had no idea she could swim that fast. Laurel struggled along in her wake, wondering desperately what they could do when they got there—if they got there in time.

There was a sudden splashing behind them. Within seconds, they had both been outdistanced by another swimmer—a man whose powerful arms and shoulders propelled him through the churning water like a torpedo.

He lifted his head and yelled, "Don't panic, kids! Just stay where you are. Everyone else keep away!"

Laurel and Goldenrod stopped swimming. All they could do was watch helplessly, treading water, as the man slowed his stroke and glided quietly up alongside Val. They saw Val point, and the man give a nod. Then he ducked his head suddenly under the water. Daisy clapped a hand to her mouth. The man's head came up. He seemed to be smiling. Val had relaxed visibly, and Daisy—could Daisy be laughing?

"Maybe there wasn't any barracuda, after all," Laurel said, mystified.

But there had been.

"You should have seen his *teeth*," Daisy said, when they were all assembled back on the beach. She stuck out her lower jaw to show what she meant.

Val turned to their rescuer—a tall, broad-shouldered man in yellow trunks, deeply tanned, and seemingly not even winded by his exertions.

"Would he really have attacked us, do you think?"

The man shrugged. "Hard to say. He was probably more curious than anything else. Barracudas aren't nearly as dangerous as sharks, unless they're provoked. But you did well to keep your heads and stay still."

"It seemed like an awful long time," Daisy said with a shiver.

"But what happened?" Goldenrod demanded of the man. "I mean, what did you do?"

Val smiled, and Daisy giggled. "He stuck his head under the water and said *Boo!* And the barracuda just turned and swam away."

The man looked a little sheepish. "Well, I've heard the island people say that barracudas are scared of loud noises. Seemed worth a try, anyway."

"Well, I'm glad it worked," Laurel said fervently.

Val said, "I thought of trying to hit him over the head with my snorkel. But with those teeth—" He shuddered. "I guess he would probably just have snapped it in two. I'm sure glad you came along when you did, sir. I mean— well, thanks a whole lot."

The man slapped him lightly on the shoulder. "Got kids of my own," he said. "You get used to keeping an eye out. Especially around water. I'd stay in close to shore for a while now," he added. "Just to be on the safe side."

But no one felt much like going back in swimming just yet.

Daisy said, "Are you having your vacation here? With your children? And your wife?"

Something wistful in her tone made the man smile down at her and gently ruffle her damp curls. "Well, not my wife," he said casually. "We're divorced. But the kids usually spend vacations down here with me. We have a lot of fun, fishing and sailing and biking around the island . . ." He glanced at the sun, low now over the shining water. "Which reminds me, I've got to get back to Marigot now and pick them up. So long, kids—nice meeting you."

He turned away, dismissing their thanks with a wave of his hand, and strode off up the beach.

"Gosh," Daisy said, gazing after him. "What a nice kind of Daddy to have."

There was a little silence. Then Heath shrugged. "Rich anyway. I mean, vacations here, and everything."

"That's not what I mean!" Daisy said. "I mean—"

She couldn't say what she meant, but they all knew. Laurel saw her eyes begin to fill with tears. "Daisy—" she began.

But Goldenrod, who had been rummaging through the beach bag for her watch, suddenly exclaimed: "Oh, good grief! Look what time it is! Listen, kids, we've got to go—right *now.*"

For in another fifteen minutes or so, Mrs. Madder would be turning into the snowy driveway at home, opening the door, calling to the children. . . . If they hurried, there would be just enough time to get out of their wet suits, and to use Mrs. Madder's hair drier—the girls, anyway—

"Susan, quick!" Goldenrod sank down cross-legged on a towel. "Sit down and start concentrating."

Susan stared around in dismay. "But what about our clothes? And Christophe? We can't just—"

"Yes, we can. We have to!"

Goldenrod pulled Susan down beside her. Reluctantly Susan crossed her legs and folded her arms across her chest. Sitting motionless as a pair of Buddhas, their wet skins gleaming gold in the last rays of the sun, they closed their eyes.

III

The sea darkened; the air turned chill; the island fell away. . . .

At least, as Heath said afterwards—rather gruesomely —no one in Grande Case could seriously believe they'd drowned. In that transparent water, you'd have no trouble spotting a dead body, let alone *six* dead bodies. And as for their clothes—well, as Daisy pointed out, they were last summer's clothes and getting too small, anyway. Val was pleased that he still had his mask and snorkel; and if Mrs. Madder ever noticed the loss of her gardening hat, she never mentioned it.

She did speak to them later that evening, rather sharply, about tracking water all over the living room. "Please remember to use the back door, children, and leave your wet things in the kitchen. Though what *anyone* was doing outside on a day like this is beyond me!"

Chapter 10 Heath's Trip

Heath knew exactly where he wanted to go. The problem was getting anyone else to go with him. Not that he really needed anybody except Goldenrod; but she was just as aghast as the rest of them.

"The Himalayas?" she said, in disbelief. "You mean those great big high mountains where it's always forty below and it never stops snowing? Where Mount Everest is?"

"Well, we wouldn't wind up on Everest necessarily," Heath assured her. "And we wouldn't go up really high. I mean, we couldn't, not without oxygen."

"Oh, my gosh!" Goldenrod stared at him. Then she pointed out the window, where the snow lay in a fat mound on top of a barberry bush. "Look, if it's snow you want, there's plenty around here."

"Or if it's mountains," said Laurel, who knew Heath better, "wouldn't an Alp do just as well? I bet there's an Alp that begins with *H*, and that wouldn't be so—well, so lonely and far away. Maybe we could even go skiing. Wait, I'll get the atlas—"

But Heath shook his head. There was a distant look in his eyes that they recognized all too well. In his mind, Heath was already poised upon a peak in the high Himalayas, treading where no man had ever trod before.

Val said, "You don't even know anything about mountain climbing. I mean, that's not the kind of stuff you can just fool around with, Heath. You need special equipment—ropes and boots and those ice-pick things—"

"Ice axes," Heath said dreamily. "And pitons and crampons and a primus stove—"

"What's he talking about?" Goldenrod demanded wildly.

Heath took in their appalled faces and came down to earth. "Well, we wouldn't have to do any climbing," he said with a sigh. "Of course we might want to walk around some, just to keep warm. . . . But the main thing is just to *be* there. I might never get another chance," he added, with a look of appeal.

During the days that followed, they tried all kinds of arguments and persuasion, but Heath wouldn't budge. It was the Himalayas or nothing. Laurel racked her brains for other *H* places Heath might like. There was Hawaii, of course, and Hong Kong—but those were islands, and they'd just been to an island. There was Hannibal, Missouri (Heath loved *Huckleberry Finn*) —but Heath said it was probably all built up by now, and anyway winter was the wrong time of year for riding

114

a raft down the Mississippi. In desperation, Laurel suggested Helsinki because of the fiords. Heath said the fiords were in Norway, not Finland, he thought everybody knew that; and anyhow, what was a fiord compared to a Himalaya?

Susan said what if they got lost, and what if they met an Abominable Snowman? Heath said there was no such thing, the Abominable Snowman was probably just a large bear or gorilla or something. (Susan swallowed hard.) As for getting lost—well, he'd take his compass, but what difference would it make, anyhow? If they got into difficulties, they could just come home.

Daisy said what if they got frostbite and their noses fell off? Heath offered to lend her his knitted facemask, but added that if it was a sunny day they were more likely to get sunburned than frostbitten. That started Goldenrod worrying about snowblindness, until Heath reminded her that all they had to do was remember to take their dark glasses. He also dealt with the problem of avalanches (which nobody had even thought of) by saying that they were very unusual at this time of year.

And so it happened that on a rather warm day of January thaw, with icicles melting outside the windows, Goldenrod and the five Madder children assembled in the living room in their warmest clothes. They wore boots and ski pants and extra sweaters under their parkas and mittens and earmuffs and scarves . . . indeed, they were so bundled up they could scarcely move.

"Whew!" said Susan. "Somebody open a window— I'm roasting!"

"You've got too many clothes on," Heath told her. "We all have. Real mountaineers don't wear all this heavy stuff. They wear layers of light clothing, and a waterproof jacket, or maybe that special cloth the astronauts' suits are made of—"

"We're not astronauts *or* mountaineers," Goldenrod reminded him. "And we may not stay there more than about ten minutes if I don't like the looks of the place." Seeing Heath's face fall, she relented enough to add "Well, we'll see what the weather's like."

Certainly it was the weather they all remembered afterwards—the weather, and the footprints. . . .

They thought they had gotten used to sudden changes of scene; but nothing had prepared them for the glittering, inhuman splendor of this new world in which they found themselves. They might not have been very high (about eight thousand feet, Heath thought), but from where they stood on the side of their own particular Himalaya, they could see nothing but mountains—peak after peak receding into the distance, flung up like frozen waves against the intense blue of the sky.

And nothing moved in all this icy wilderness. There was no sign of any living creatures except themselves; nor any sound, except for a curious high-pitched humming noise, like the sound of high-tension wires. After a moment they realized it was only the voice of the wind, singing to itself here at the lonely top of the world.

They themselves were protected from the wind by what Heath said was a spur of the mountain—a great sheer hump of rock and ice that loomed high above the snowfield in which they stood. This was shaped like a shallow tilted bowl; it caught and held the brilliant mountain sunshine like a giant reflector.

"It's not even cold here," Laurel marveled. "Or if it is, it doesn't feel like it."

It was true. The air was so dry that you couldn't really feel the cold, except as a kind of tingling sensation. And the snow was dry, too, fine and powdery; it squeaked under their boots. When Val tried to make a snowball, the snow didn't even stick to his mittens.

"Oh, I wish we had our sleds!" Daisy's eyes shone through the slits of Heath's face mask as she surveyed the dazzling, unmarked expanse of snow before them.

"Wow, what a place to get a tan!" Goldenrod threw back the hood of her emerald-green parka and lifted her face to the sun. "Imagine coming all the way to the Himalayas to sunbathe—crazy! This isn't at all the way I thought it would be," she added. "I bet it's almost as nice as Sun Valley."

"Maybe you better keep your hood on, though," Susan said nervously. "Or wear my earmuffs, at least." As she spoke she glanced over her shoulder at the great bulk of the spur. She couldn't help wondering what (or *who*) might be lurking on the other side.

Heath, too, was studying the spur, but for different reasons. "Maybe we should explore a little," he said. "I mean, as long as we're here."

"Not all the way up there!" Laurel said, following his glance. "Anyway, we couldn't climb that, Heath. It's much too steep."

"Well—no," Heath said reluctantly. "But if we worked our way across a little—over that way—maybe we could get to see more of the mountain."

The mountain they were on, he meant. It was true that they couldn't see much of it from where they stood and nothing at all of the peak somewhere high above them. Laurel looked where Heath was pointing. It appeared to be an easy enough walk—diagonally across the snowfield to the point where it joined a long, gently sloping ridge.

Daisy, who was making a series of angels in the snow, didn't want to go exploring, and neither did Goldenrod. She had settled herself comfortably against a small hummock and had her eyes closed. "I never did have a chance to sunbathe in St. Martin," she said drowsily. "One of the girls at work went to Florida over Christmas, and you should see how tan she got."

Susan wondered if Goldenrod could be coming down with snow sickness already. She'd read about people falling asleep in the snow and freezing to death. But before she could say anything, Laurel said, "Well, my feet are beginning to get a little cold, and I think Heath's right—we ought to keep moving."

"*And* we ought to stick together," Heath declared. "That's the first rule in the mountains."

He picked up the hickory branch he'd brought along in lieu of an ice axe, settled his pack more comfortably between his shoulder blades, and started off. No one knew what was in the pack. "Provisions," Heath had said importantly, rummaging around in the kitchen cupboards at home.

Daisy lay down flat on her back, moved her arms slowly and carefully to make one last perfect snow angel, and scampered off after Heath. Goldenrod got up with a sigh, dusted off the back of her green parka, and fell into step with Susan and Val. Val didn't say much as they walked along; but then, he never did. Susan noticed, however, that he kept glancing up at the top of the spur to their right with a preoccupied air.

"What's the matter?" she asked worriedly. "What do you see?"

"Oh—just a cloud," he said. "It's sort of funny-look-ing, though."

Susan shrugged. She certainly wasn't afraid of *clouds*.

They trudged on across the snowfield, which was a good deal wider than they'd realized. Footing was no problem, but they were glad of their sunglasses in the dazzle that struck up at them from all sides as they walked.

By the time they reached the ridge, they were warm with exertion, and the last few yards were a scramble. They arrived panting at the top, eager to see what they could see.

"Darn!" said Heath.

Before them lay another snowfield and another ridge. To their right, the mass of the great spur still blocked their view of the higher slopes of the mountain. Now Susan noticed the cloud Val had mentioned—a gray swirl that was blotting out a small section of blue sky. It wasn't very big, but it seemed to grow bigger as she looked at it.

"Let's try the next ridge," Heath said, and before any-one could argue with him, he was setting off across the second snowfield.

They looked at each other and shrugged. There was less protection from the wind here; they decided they might as well keep moving.

Their pace was slower now, as the altitude began to affect them a little. Their hearts thumped, their breath-ing was shallow, and they felt slightly giddy—though that might have been the affect of the glare.

Heath reached the second ridge first and stood shak-ing his head in disappointment. More of the mountain was visible from here, but the peak was still hidden. The others clambered up beside him, less interested now in the view than in the chance to rest.

"Brr," said Susan. "Let's get out of the wind."

The sun still shone as brightly as before, but now the wind had an edge to it. The gray cloud had grown much larger, Susan noticed, looking around at the spur. They found a sheltered ledge just below the spine of the ridge and sat down to catch their breaths.

"I'm thirsty," Daisy announced, looking at Heath's pack. "What did you bring to drink, Heath?"

Heath opened his pack and produced two tins of sardines, six oranges, and six small squares of chocolate. They stared at this collection in dismay.

"Sardines!" said Laurel. "*Ugh!* You know nobody likes sardines, Heath."

"High protein," Heath explained. "And the chocolate's for energy. Real mountaineers have special rations, of course—but the idea is to travel light and get the most out of your food. The oranges weren't so light," he admitted, when nobody said anything, "but they're good for you. And the juice is for when you're thirsty."

Daisy said, "But isn't there even any water?"

"Gosh," Val said, "I could have brought my canteen, at least."

They all looked reproachfully at Heath, who said, "You don't want to drink a lot of water in the mountains. It just weighs you down. Hey, don't do that!" Daisy had scooped up a handful of snow and was about to put it in her mouth. "If you eat snow, it just makes you thirstier."

Goldenrod said, "He's right about that, Daisy. Have an orange instead." She reached for a tin of sardines and began opening it. "Anyway, *I* like sardines, even if nobody else does."

She offered the tin around, but they shuddered and shook their heads. "Besides," Susan said, "they'll just make you thirstier."

"Then I'll have an orange," Goldenrod said cheerfully.

The trouble with the oranges, they discovered, was that you had to take off your mittens to peel them; and suddenly the air seemed to have grown much colder.

While they ate, Heath paced restlessly along the ledge, looking up at the mountain. The slope nearest them was steep and rugged, crisscrossed by gullies and crevices. It ended in an overhang which cut off all but a glimpse of another, gentler-looking slope beyond. Probably the overhang could be climbed, Heath thought wistfully, if only you knew how.

Val joined him, munching the last of his chocolate. "What about that cloud?" he said, pointing. "Do you think it's going to snow?"

"Oh, it's still a long way off," Heath replied absently. He was studying the line of the ridge they were on, seeing how it met the spur at the point where the spur joined the main mass of the mountain. It wouldn't be much of a climb—and once you were up on the shoulder of the mountain, maybe the peak would be visible. . . .

"Where are you going?" Val demanded, as Heath started back up onto the top of the ridge.

"I just want to get a little closer," Heath said.

"Not without the rest of us," Val told him firmly. "You were the one who said we ought to stick together, remember?"

121

They were all chilled from sitting and glad enough to get moving again. Quickly they packed up the remains of the meal and followed Heath along the top of the ridge.

The going was harder here, on this exposed surface. There were half-frozen drifts carved by the wind and icy patches concealed by a thin coating of snow. As they moved closer into the mountain, the ridge narrowed, and the drop became steeper on both sides. It no longer looked like good sledding country; in fact, they decided as they picked their way along, it was probably better not to look down at all.

The ridge began angling upward to meet the spur. Instinctively they moved into single file, their heads bent against the knifelike wind. Heath, in the lead, was walking cautiously now, prodding the snow ahead with his stick at each step.

"Where is this wind coming from, anyway?" Goldenrod said breathlessly. "You'd think the mountain would cut it off."

Laurel, behind her, had been thinking the same thing. The sunlight had gone, now that they were in the shadow of the mountain—or was it a cloud instead that had blotted it out? She squinted upward and could see no blue sky at all any more, only a swirl of gray.

"Heath!" she called. "I don't think we'd better go any farther. It's going to snow!"

As she spoke, the first few light flakes brushed their cheeks. At the same moment, Heath gave a shout, and they saw where the wind was coming from. There was a narrow, V-shaped notch in the spur, just at the point where it joined the mountain. This was acting like a funnel for the wind—and now for the snow as well, which was driving horizontally into their faces.

"Come on!" Goldenrod said. "Let's get out of this!"

She moved into the shelter of the spur itself, edging along the face of a great slab of rock streaked with black ice. The others followed—all except Heath.

"I'm going up!" they heard him yell over the wind. "It's easy from here."

Val peered around the side of the slab, blinking into the gusting snow. He saw that Heath had already reached the bottom of the notch and was starting up the steep lefthand slope which would bring him out onto the shoulder of the mountain above.

"Be careful!" he called; but his words were torn back over his shoulder by the wind. He waited long enough to see that Heath was climbing steadily but slowly up the incline, feeling carefully for handholds and setting his feet firmly before each upward thrust of his body.

"He's okay, I guess," Val reported, rejoining the others. "It's steep, but it's not very far."

It was snowing much harder now. The wind howled over the top of the spur and whined through crevices; it tossed up spumes of snow like ocean spray from drifts and hollows. They flattened themselves against the rock as the flakes whirled and danced before them. They could no longer see more than a few hundred feet of the long ridge they had traversed and nothing at all of the gentle snowfields far below.

"Even if Heath does get up there," Laurel said with a shiver, "he won't be able to see anything."

"I wish he'd come back," Goldenrod said. Her face in the emerald-green hood was pinched with cold and anxiety. "Val, go see where he is now."

123

But it was almost impossible to make out anything in the torrent of wind and snow that was streaming through the gap. For a terrible moment, Val thought the wind might have blown Heath clear off the mountain. Then he caught a glimpse of Heath's red parka high above him. He had reached the top of the V and was moving on up the mountain—slowly crouched low against the force of the wind, but climbing doggedly and steadily upward; as if, Val thought, he intended to go all the way up to the peak itself.

Val waited for a lull in the storm, and then yelled through his cupped hands, "Heath! Come back here!"

The small figure paused. Val yelled again. Even from here Val could see Heath's reluctance to turn back. But at last he did. Val saw him begin to retrace his steps, before a fresh blast of snow blotted him from sight.

Val ducked back into the comparative shelter of the slab. "He's coming. But of all the crazy things to do!" Angrily he brushed the crusted snow from his eyelashes with his sleeve. "Climbing a mountain in the middle of a blizzard—I ask you!"

Daisy said in a small voice, "Isn't it time to go home yet?"

"We can't, not till Heath gets back," Susan pointed out. "Anyway, it's his trip, and if he wants to go climbing—"

She broke off suddenly. "What's *that?*" she said in a hushed, fearful voice.

They squinted through the snow. With a shaking mittened hand, Susan was pointing at the shallow basin just below them. A line of footprints crossed it at an angle, leading from the direction of the ridge on their right and disappearing around an outcrop some distance to their left. They were fresh footprints, not yet erased by the new snow, and very large.

"One of us must have made them," Laurel said, with more assurance than she felt.

"But nobody's been down there!" Susan wailed.

"Well, if Heath went exploring along the way—" Goldenrod began, her own voice sounding shaky.

"He didn't!" said Susan. "I was right behind him, and he stayed on top of the ridge the whole time. And anyway, look how *big* they are! Oh!" she moaned. "It's here! It's somewhere right around! And it's watching us—I can feel it . . . Oh! Oh!"

"Susan!" Goldenrod spoke sharply.

Susan was staring around wildly. In another moment she might have dashed away from them, plunging off into the storm in her terror. Goldenrod reached out to grab her arm—and then they heard Heath's shout.

"Help!"

It came to them very faintly, no more than a muffled cry blown by the wind.

Slipping and floundering in the fresh snow, they worked their way around the face of the slab. The open V of the notch was almost invisible now in the swirling snow, but Heath's red parka stood out clearly. He was braced in the angle of the V, his back pressed against one side and his feet against the other. Below him there was only empty space.

"Don't come any closer!" he yelled, as they started forward. "It's just a snow bridge—not solid!"

They stared in horror. What had appeared to be the firm base of the notch was now a yawning gap where a great chunk of snow had broken off. It was easy enough to see what had happened. Under the fresh snowfall and the extra weight of Heath's descent, the bridge had given way—and now only the pressure of Heath's body was holding him above the gap.

"Heath!" Goldenrod called against the wind. "Don't move! I'm going to try to get us home."

Would it work without Heath? They didn't know. Laurel thought of Gorseville—oh, the blessed heat of Gorseville!—and of how Goldenrod had taken them there and back on her own. But this wasn't a G place; it was Heath's trip. And Heath. . . .

They waited tensely as Goldenrod sat down cross-legged in the snow, her eyes squeezed shut, fighting grimly for the way back. A long minute passed, in which the only sound was the shrieking of the wind through the notch.

Then Goldenrod shook her head and got to her feet. "If only I had more time," she said despairingly.

But they looked at Heath and knew that time was just what they didn't have. He couldn't possibly hold the strain of his position much longer, buffeted as he was by the full force of the wind.

Val had been studying the face of the right-hand slope, the side supporting Heath's back and shoulders. Now he bent down and quickly brushed some snow from what they saw was a projecting ledge. It was no more than a foot wide, but it looked solid—and it extended along the face as far as they could see.

Val said urgently, "Even if it doesn't go all the way—if we had something we could throw."

Goldenrod saw his idea immediately. She snatched the long woolen scarf from around Susan's neck and gave it to him.

"Everybody join hands," she ordered. "Val, be careful!"

Val was already moving out along the ledge, his back
flattened against the slope. Laurel joined him, and they
clasped hands firmly. Goldenrod came next, then Susan
and Daisy, until they were all strung out upon the narrow ledge like cutout paper dolls—and feeling almost
as fragile.

Step by step, they began to inch sideways as Val felt
his way cautiously along the ledge. When he reached
the point where the snow bridge had given way, he told
himself not to look down—not to look anywhere, in fact,
not even at Heath. He concentrated instead on his footing, scraping at the snow with the toe of his boot, testing
the ledge at each step before shifting his weight. The
wind tore at his clothes, and the right side of his face
had gone numb.

Heath watched tensely, turning his head as much as
he dared. His shoulders ached, and his knees were beginning to tremble; but he tried not to think about
them. Val was five feet away now, and then only four
. . . and there the ledge ended.

Val's boot almost slid off the edge, but Laurel's quick
tug at his arm held him firm against the slope.

Heath said in a quavering voice, "I don't think I can
reach you from there."

"This is close enough," Val told him and hoped it was
true. "Now listen, Heath—I'm going to toss this scarf to
you. Stretch out your arm a little, if you can, but don't
move any more than you have to. When you've got a
good grip on it, I'll give you a signal, and you take a
giant step sideways. We'll all be holding you, so don't

worry." He managed a grin. "A rescue party, right? Just like in real mountaineering."

"Except for not having a rope," Heath said; but his voice sounded a little stronger.

"Okay, everybody, hang on!" Val called. He flung the end of the scarf toward Heath's outstretched hand. The wind caught it and blew it back.

"No!" Val said sharply, as Heath shifted his shoulders in an effort to bring himself closer. "Don't move! I'll try again."

He waited for a lull in the wind, flexing his cold fingers inside his gloves, and hoping that Heath still had some feeling in his hands. When the wind dropped for a moment, he tossed the scarf out again—and this time Heath caught it.

"Okay," Val yelled. *"Now!"*

He gave a mighty tug, and Heath lunged sideways. His boot scrabbled for the tip of the ledge. For a horrifying moment it looked as though he would fall—and could they hold him then? But the human chain leaned and pulled and held firm; and in another instant, Heath had been dragged onto the safety of the ledge.

He stood panting and shivering, his eyes closed. Val himself was trembling, but he said, "Better not rest yet, Heath—your muscles will just stiffen up, and we still have to get off the ledge."

Slowly and painfully, but with more confidence now, they inched their way back along the ledge to solid ground.

"Well," said Goldenrod, as they stood together in an exhausted huddle. "I don't know about anyone else, but I say it's time we went home."

And for once no one argued with her—though Heath

gave a last glance upward at the invisible peak, hidden from him forever now by the storm and by the distance that would soon separate them. His eyes were taking on their faraway gleam, his ordeal already forgotten. Next time, he promised himself, I'll have an ice axe and pitons and crampons; and a good strong rope. . . .

Later, when they were talking it all over, Susan said reproachfully to Goldenrod, "I thought you were getting better about details. I mean, it wasn't your fault if St. Martin was so crowded with tourists and everything. But those horrible footprints!" She shuddered. "And after you promised me you wouldn't even think about the Abominable Snowman!"

Goldenrod looked blank. "But I didn't. I couldn't have. I mean, I don't *believe* in the Abominable Snowman—so how could I have been thinking about him?"

"Then," said Laurel slowly, "whose footprints were they?"

Chapter 11 *Daisy's Trip*

Goldenrod had been the Madders' baby-sitter for almost six months now, and Mrs. Madder's only worry was that she might suddenly decide to leave. She told herself this was silly, when everything seemed to be going so well. Still, there was something about the girl . . . she never seemed quite in focus, somehow. "I can't get her outlines clear," was the way Mrs. Madder put it to herself, as if Goldenrod were the subject of a painting.

Mrs. Madder was painting a good deal these days and feeling quite satisfied with the results—though some of the pictures continued to baffle her. Why should she have wanted to paint a tropical seascape, for instance, with all those palm trees and fishing boats and pelicans? It had been a terrible struggle to keep it from looking like an over-colored tourist's postcard. More recently, she'd found herself painting a large canvas white—layers and layers of white paint, with only a few scattered blobs of color, a bit of red here, some green there. . . . It wasn't her sort of thing at all, Mrs. Madder thought irritably. Yet somehow it demanded to be finished before she could go on to anything else.

When Heath came up to the attic one day, she saw him eyeing these new paintings with a startled look. Then his expression changed; for a moment Mrs. Madder thought he was going to burst out laughing. But when she asked him what was so funny, he only shook his head and said he couldn't explain.

The children did seem to have a lot of secrets these days, Mrs. Madder thought. There were sudden explosions of giggles and conversations that broke off abruptly when she entered a room. Some game they were playing with Goldenrod, she decided—or maybe a project they were working on as a surprise for her. Little did Mrs. Madder know how surprised she was going to be, one day quite soon.

Then the atmosphere changed. Instead of giggles, there were whispered arguments, and a feeling of tension in the house when Mrs. Madder came home at night. This awful month of February she thought with a sigh; it seems like the longest month of the year instead of the shortest, as if winter would never end. No wonder the children felt cooped-up and cranky—too slushy outside for sledding and skating, too cold for bike riding, too soon for baseball. . . . Mrs. Madder began work on a painting of an empty ballpark in the rain.

But of course the real problem wasn't the weather; it was Daisy's trip. The others had made lists of interesting D places for her, figuring that Daisy might not have any ideas of her own—or if she did, she'd come up with something like a visit to the local Dairy Queen. They pooled the lists and decided that Disneyland was their best bet; or Disney World, maybe, the one in Florida. Daisy would be sure to choose one or the other.

But Daisy did have an idea of her own—a very definite one. "I want to go see Daddy," she declared.

The others exchanged glances. "I know," Laurel said gently. "But that's not a place, Daisy, it's a person. You have to choose a *place* beginning with *D*."

Daisy said, "But I do have a place. Danbury, Connecticut."

They stared at her. Daisy's face was flushed, and her eyes were shining.

"I saw the envelope," she explained. "I always look at the envelopes Mother gets, just in case. And that's where Daddy's living now. He was in New York before, and of course I couldn't get *there*. But Danbury's easy. So that's where we'll go."

She gave a little nod of satisfaction, as if it were all settled.

"But Daisy, he won't even know—" Heath began, but stopped as Laurel shook her head at him.

They all knew what Heath was going to say: that their father probably wouldn't know who Daisy was even if she walked right up to him. He had left before she was born and had never seen her. Of course there had been family snapshots over the years—but they weren't very good snapshots, usually rather blurry and underexposed. Mrs. Madder disliked cameras and had never really learned to use one. But even if their father *did* recognize Daisy and the rest of them—

"It'll just get her all upset," Laurel said later, when Daisy had gone over to a friend's house to play. "She'll want him to come home—and of course he won't, not after all this time."

"And what if he's mean to her?" Heath demanded. "He probably doesn't even *like* kids."

"He's probably just an old grouch," Susan agreed.

Val and Laurel smiled at each other, a little sadly. They remembered their father as a vague, kindly man who seemed bewildered by his children. He disliked noise and confusion, but he never lost his temper. Instead he retreated, usually to the basement where he had his studio. They remembered the smell of damp clay and plaster, the bare light bulb overhead, and most of all their father's hands—so clumsy and uncertain at ordinary tasks, so sure and strong at his work.

But of course Heath and Susan had been too young to remember their father as more than a dim presence in the background of their lives.

"Well, *I* certainly don't want him to come back," Susan was saying vehemently. "I don't care if we never see him again!" But her voice quavered a little on the last words.

"Yeah," Heath said. "If he doesn't want us, we sure don't want him, either."

Laurel shook her head. "That isn't the point," she said. "He won't be coming back. But if we do get to see him—well, I'm just afraid Daisy will be disappointed."

They mulled the problem over among themselves for several days. Meanwhile Daisy went around humming happily to herself and spent hours in front of her closet, deciding what she would wear to impress her unknown father. She was sure that if he saw how pretty she was, he would love her and want to come home. Finally Laurel decided to talk to Goldenrod about it.

But Goldenrod's reaction surprised her. "I think Daisy should go," she said firmly. "Whatever happens, she needs to find out about her father for herself. It isn't good, the way you kids never talk about him."

"But mother—"

"Maybe your mother doesn't realize how Daisy's built the whole thing up in her mind. Maybe she has her own reasons for not talking about your father." She looked at Laurel thoughtfully. "Do you think she's still in love with him?"

Laurel stared. In love . . . her mother? She took it for granted that her parents had loved each other when they got married; but after all these years—

Goldenrod shrugged. "I just wondered. Like she never got married again, and she doesn't seem to have any boyfriends hanging around. . . ."

But this was too much for Laurel. Her mother having boyfriends? She began to giggle. Then she sobered again at the thought of Daisy going off to search for her long-lost father, like some poor orphan in a fairy tale. Or maybe it was the thought of seeing him again herself that was really bothering her. How would she feel about it? Laurel realized she didn't know.

As if she sensed Laurel's confusion, Goldenrod said casually, "It's going to be kind of strange for you, too, I guess—meeting up with your dad again. Of course the rest of you could just stay out of sight while Daisy does her thing." She gave a shrug. "Anyway, who knows? We may not even find him."

And this was very nearly true. They were all ready to set off for Danbury when Goldenrod asked if Daisy remembered the street address on the envelope.

She didn't; and none of them wanted to go prying among their mother's things.

"Well, then—" Val began hopefully. He was about to point out that Danbury was a pretty big town—a small city, in fact—and that the chances of finding their father would be slim indeed without an address to go on.

But Daisy said cheerfully, "Oh, we can look him up in the phone book."

The others looked at each other. If their father had just moved there, his name probably wouldn't be in the phone book yet. But no one had the heart to say anything. Daisy was wearing her new white blouse with her good plaid skirt and its matching jacket. Her socks were very clean, and her shoes were polished. On her lap she held the shiny red pocketbook that Laurel had given her for Christmas.

"We'll go to Main Street first," she informed Goldenrod. "And then we'll ask directions, the way we did in Gorseville."

"What if there isn't any Main Street?" Goldenrod said. She was beginning to sound a little nervous herself.

Daisy said confidently, "Oh, there will be. Places *have* to have a Main Street. How would people find their way around if they didn't?"

With which she sat up very straight in her chair, crossed her arms and legs neatly, and closed her eyes. Her small face was calm and expectant. With a sigh, Goldenrod followed suit.

Laurel felt suddenly panicky. No! she thought. I don't

135

want to go! This is a mistake. Maybe I can fight against it. If I concentrate as hard as I can on staying right here at home. . . .

But already her eyelids were growing heavy. She wanted to open them and couldn't. She tried to hold her body stiff, resisting the soft pull, the slow drag of distance. But it was no good. She could feel herself beginning to drift; and now she was sliding, sliding away. . . .

Daisy was right. There *was* a Main Street in Danbury, Connecticut—a long Main Street, busy with traffic and shoppers on this late-February afternoon. The weather was mild but cloudy; people carried umbrellas and glanced up from time to time at the murky sky.

"Well, here we are," Goldenrod said, surveying the scene without enthusiasm.

It certainly wasn't the most exciting-looking place they'd seen on their travels. But of course they hadn't come for the scenery. They were scanning the store fronts for a drugstore that would have a phone directory, when Daisy gave a triumphant cry.

"They'll know in here," she said; and before anyone could stop her, she had darted into a small art supply store. Through the window they could see her talking eagerly to the elderly proprietor. After a moment he nodded—a bit grimly, it seemed—and began writing something down on a scrap of paper.

"Maybe he won't be home," Heath suggested. He sounded torn between hope and anxiety.

"Well, whether he is or not," Susan said, "let's hope it isn't very far. I just heard some thunder."

"Thunder? At this time of year?" Heath scoffed.

"Well, I did! And it looks like it's going to pour rain any minute."

They were still arguing about this when Daisy came running out of the store, waving the scrap of paper. "He knows Daddy, all right," she reported happily. "And Daddy doesn't have a phone, so it's a good thing I went in there. The man says Daddy owes him some money and will we please remind him about it." For a moment her face fell. "Oh," she said, "I hope Daddy isn't really *poor!*"

"Probably he just forgot," Laurel told her, with a dim memory of discussions about bills her father never got around to opening.

Goldenrod was studying the little map the man had sketched. "It looks easy enough," she said. "We turn right and then left after a few blocks and go down toward the railroad tracks." She shook her head. "Sounds like a funny place for an artist to pick."

Laurel thought so, too, remembering how her father had felt about noise. But she said nothing, following the others around a corner onto the side street marked on the map. The afternoon seemed darker than ever, away from the lights of Main Street. Susan insisted again that she heard thunder, but Heath said it was probably just a train going by.

And indeed, as they approached the address the man had given Daisy, they could see a railroad crossing ahead. Suddenly red lights flashed, a gate came down across the street, and a freight train began rumbling slowly along the tracks. Heath, who loved freights because of the names on the tracks—Great Northern, Baltimore & Ohio, Union Pacific—slowed down to count them.

"Sixteen, seventeen, eighteen," he was mumbling, as Susan tugged at his arm. "Nineteen, twenty, twenty-one . . . gosh, it's a long one! Twenty-two, twenty-three—"

"Heath!" Susan said. "We're here."

Heath looked around. "We are? Where?"

Narrow three-story houses lined both sides of the street. Many of them had small stores or businesses on the ground level. There was a pizza parlor, an optician's, a shoe repair store, an insurance agency. Susan was pointing to the house nearest the tracks on their side of the street. "Joe Pye's Italian Market" said the sign over the front door.

The freight train was still going by. Heath gave it a last reluctant look before he trailed the others into the grocery store. It smelled of cheese and onions and Italian sausage—good, strong, spicy smells. There was fresh sawdust on the floor, and the fruits and vegetables in their bins looked as if they had been lovingly polished that afternoon.

Goldenrod was talking to a round-faced man in a clean white butcher's apron—Joe Pye himself. He was shaking his head dubiously.

"He doesn't like to be disturbed when he's working," he explained. "Could be the President himself, Mr. Madder'd just tell him to come back later."

Daisy whispered to Laurel, "Is *this* where Daddy lives?" She looked around in bewilderment.

"Upstairs, I guess," Laurel said. It certainly did seem like an odd place to choose.

Mr. Pye said, "Well—I guess it won't do no harm to try, if you want to go on up." He had been absent-mindedly polishing apples with his apron as he spoke.

Now he handed one to each of them and gave Daisy an extra.

"You take him up an apple, young lady," he said, smiling at her. "He usually forgets to have lunch, so he's probably kind of hungry by now."

They thanked him and edged around the meat counter to the door he indicated at the back of the store. It led to a narrow stairway, dimly lighted. When they came to the first landing, Goldenrod shook her head. "This is where the Pyes live," she said. "Your father's on the top floor."

Silently they climbed another flight, which ended abruptly at a closed door. Over the departing rumble of the freight train, they could hear a faint tapping sound —but that was all.

Goldenrod nodded at Daisy, who stood holding her two apples, looking suddenly very small and lost and scared. "Maybe we better not," she whispered uncertainly. "Maybe he'll be mad."

They stood crowded together on the top steps, awkward and undecided.

Then Laurel made up her mind. She leaned past Daisy and knocked loudly on the door.

"Father!" she called. "It's Laurel."

"And Val," Val said.

"And all the rest of us," Heath put in bravely.

The tapping sound had stopped. Now there was only silence.

"It's your *children*!" Susan yelled suddenly in an angry voice.

For a moment nothing happened. Then they heard footsteps The door opened, letting out a stream of gray light, and their father stood before them—a tall man in dusty workclothes, blinking tired eyes at them from behind his glasses. His expression was polite, but puzzled. Did he even remember that he had children?"

"I brought you an apple," Daisy said in a shaky voice, holding it out to him.

"An apple," Mr. Madder repeated slowly. He took it from her and stood turning it over in his hand. "It's a beautiful apple," he said; and they saw that it was, glowing like a jewel in the pale, dusty light. Their father looked from the apple to Daisy, standing there so still and anxious in her good clothes. The beginnings of a smile transformed his face.

"And you," he said, "are Daisy. Thank you, Daisy."

At which Daisy threw her arms around his waist and burst into tears.

"What's this, what's this?" he said, absently patting the top of her head. He nodded at the rest of his family. "Well, come in, all of you, come in."

They filed into the big room and stood looking around curiously. Tall windows filled one wall, and there was a skylight overhead. Even on this murky day, the place seemed full of light. A long scarred workbench ran beneath the windows, and there was a narrow bed against one wall. The only other furniture consisted of a small round table, a battered armchair, a bookcase, and a cabinet full of sculptor's tools. In the middle of the room, a large chunk of white stone stood on a dropcloth, with a chisel and hammer lying nearby.

"I try to keep things tidy," Mr. Madder said with a sigh. "But now that I'm working in marble—the dust, you see . . ."

Actually the room would have been immaculate, except for its fine coating of marble dust. There were only a few small pieces of sculpture about, and a single painting over the rough fireplace that Laurel thought might be one of their mother's. She glimpsed a half-open door in a corner to what looked like a storeroom. That must be where her father kept his finished work

"It's a very nice place," Heath said politely.

His father looked at him intently for a moment. "You have your mother's eyes," he said. "Extraordinary. . . . Yes, it suits me very well here. I tried living in the country at first, but there were too many distractions. Birds, you know, and grass to cut," he explained. "And then, when they decided to tear down the warehouse in New York—that was a good place, except for the soot—I came here. Convenient, you know, with Joe downstairs. I don't even have to go out to shop."

Laurel had been wondering where the kitchen was. Now she spied a small alcove behind a screen, with a two-burner stove, a tiny sink, and a refrigerator.

Val had wandered over to the big windows, which overlooked the railroad tracks. "It must get pretty noisy here, though," he said. "With all the trains going by."

As he spoke, there was a distant rumble. Another freight approaching? No, it was thunder, after all. They saw a distant flare of lightning.

"Ah, but that's an impersonal kind of noise," his father said, taking a bite of his apple. "It's not a noise I have to *do* anything about," he explained.

Laurel nodded. Not like the noise of children crying or the ringing of a telephone or even a wife calling him for supper. She felt sad for her father, without knowing quite why. Certainly *he* didn't seem sad or even lonely. There was a look of peace in the mild brown eyes behind the dusty glasses.

"Well," Mr. Madder said, rousing himself with an obvious effort. He smiled at his family rather shyly. "This is quite a reunion, isn't it? Now let me see—can I offer anyone a glass of water? Or I could send down to Joe for some Cokes—"

Susan, who had been studying her father in silence, seemed suddenly to make up her mind. "No, thank you, Daddy," she said with a smile. "Water would be fine."

"I'll get it," Daisy said eagerly.

"I'm afraid there are only two glasses," their father said apologetically. "But if you don't mind taking turns . . ."

Laurel noticed that he kept glancing in a puzzled way at Goldenrod, as if wondering if she were a daughter he'd somehow forgotten about. Quickly she introduced them.

"A baby-sitter," he said, nodding. "Fine, fine. . . . I'm sure your mother can use the help." He was staring at Goldenrod thoughtfully. "An interesting bone structure," he remarked.

Goldenrod took a step backward in alarm, as if afraid he was going to approach her with his chisel.

Susan began to giggle. She caught Heath's eye, and he grinned back at her, shrugging his shoulders. "I'm sure your mother can use the help" indeed! But it was impossible to stay mad at this strange man who was their father, they realized; somehow the ordinary rules just didn't apply.

Daisy was solemnly handing the two jelly glasses of

water around. Susan took a sip, choked, and began giggling again.

A faint expression of annoyance crossed their father's face. "You children were always laughing about something," he said, more to himself than to them. "I never did understand what. Distracting, all the same . . . Well, now." He cleared his throat. "Let me hear all about you, and what you've been up to. Your mother writes to me, of course, but I'm afraid I have a bad habit of mislaying letters. Now that you've come for a visit, however. . . ."

It didn't seem to occur to him to wonder how they'd come, or how they were going to get home again. He offered the old armchair politely to Goldenrod and stood leaning against the workbench with his arms folded, patiently prepared to listen. The children sat down in a row on the bed, facing him. Laurel saw how her father's glance rested for a moment on the chunk of marble before he turned his attention back to them.

They told him dutifully about their schoolwork and their teachers, and how they were taking care of the house now that Miss Vetch had left. It was hard to tell how much of it their father took in; indeed, they had the feeling he couldn't remember who Miss Vetch was. Daisy chattered away happily about her new best friend Ivy and the secret club they'd formed (just the two of them) . She told about her class trip to the aquarium, and how she already knew her multiplication tables up to seven—

"Good, good," Mr. Madder said, nodding. "I take it you saw all the lions and bears and monkeys—"

"It was the *aquarium*, Daddy," Daisy said, puzzled. "Not the zoo."

"Ah, yes. Seals, then. And fish," Mr. Madder said vaguely.

In a very short time, the conversation began to run down. In an effort to revive it, Laurel asked if they could see some of their father's finished work—glancing hopefully at the storeroom door. But Mr. Madder just shook his head absently. Obviously it was only the new work that interested him. More and more his gaze kept returning to the piece of marble in the center of the room, as if he saw something there that no one else could see.

Val cleared his throat, breaking another silence, and said, "What other things do you do, Father? Besides working, I mean."

"Oh. . . ." Mr. Madder had to think. "Well, I take walks sometimes, and once in a while I go to the movies. I did have a car, but it broke down. It hardly seemed worth having it fixed, you know, since there's really no place I want to go."

During this exchange, Daisy had been watching her father with an unblinking stare that would have made anyone except Mr. Madder nervous. Indeed, it made the others nervous; they glanced at her uneasily. But Daisy didn't seem unhappy or upset—just thoughtful.

And now the storm was moving closer. The room had grown quite dark, and there were jagged streaks of lightning among the angry purple clouds beyond the windows. When a crack of thunder made them all jump, Goldenrod rose and said she thought they really ought to be going, before the storm broke.

Mr. Madder nodded, and everyone looked relieved. As Heath said afterwards, their father seemed pleased enough to see them; but he would have been just as pleased *not* to see them—and after a while they couldn't help feeling a little the same way.

But there was a moment, as they stood clustered in the doorway once more, when his gaze fastened on them with a sudden intensity. They felt he was really looking at them for the first time—looking at each face in turn and memorizing it, perhaps. He gave Val's shoulder a squeeze and smoothed the hair back from Laurel's forehead with a large, clumsy hand. "Good girl," he murmured.

When Daisy hugged him goodbye, he let his face rest for a moment on the top of her curly head. It was hard to tell in the dim light; but when he straightened up, they thought they saw tears in his eyes.

"It was good of you to come," he said. He paused, obviously searching for words, and then gave a helpless shrug. "I'm sorry," was all he said.

"Don't be," Susan told him. "It's all right."

She smiled up at her father; and after a moment he smiled back and bent to kiss the tip of her nose. He looked once more into Heath's eyes, said, "Remarkable," and shook hands formally with Goldenrod. The visit was over.

But as they felt their way down the narrow stairs, they knew he was still standing there in the doorway, watching them. Only when they reached the turn at the landing did they hear the door close, very gently, above them.

Chapter 12 Goldenrod's Story

"Why do we always seem to get *wet?*" Susan demanded, dripping water onto the living room rug.

But she was still smiling from the exhilaration of their wild dash through the thunderstorm. Rain or no rain, they'd all felt a sense of release after the long hour they'd spent in their father's studio. Goldenrod had had to speak to them quite sternly before she managed to herd them all up onto the shelter of somebody's front porch, where she and Daisy could arrange themselves for the trip back.

Now she shook her head reproachfully. "The way you kids were all running around and yelling, in the middle of a thunderstorm—honestly, people must have thought you were nuts!"

"People in Danbury," Heath said with a shrug. "Who cares? We'll never see *them* again. We—"

He froze. Their mother had just entered the room.

"There you are!" she exclaimed in relief. "I couldn't imagine where you'd all gone to. Funny, I didn't even hear the front door open."

It was her turn to stop dead. "But you're all wet," she said in a wondering voice. "How on earth did you get so wet?"

No one had to look out the window to know that the sun was shining brightly outside and that the pavements were dry.

Laurel faltered, "What—what are you doing home so early?"

Mrs. Madder sank into a chair, still staring at them. "I had a toothache," she said slowly, "so I went to the dentist and took the rest of the afternoon off."

Goldenrod was edging toward the front door. Her face had gone white, and her green eyes looked enormous.

Mrs. Madder noticed. "Goldenrod," she said sharply, "please come back and sit down. I think you owe me an explanation. What's been going on around here?"

She looked around the room at her children, and then back at Goldenrod, who returned very slowly to the couch and sat down on the edge of it.

Unexpectedly, Mrs. Madder began to laugh. "If you could see yourselves!" she said. "Like a bunch of drowned rats—*guilty* drowned rats. Now come on, everybody. What's the big secret? Where have you been?"

Daisy opened her mouth and closed it again. Mrs. Madder eyed her narrowly. "And why," she went on, more soberly, "is Daisy all dressed up in her good skirt? Heavens, I hope all that water hasn't ruined it."

Daisy looked down at her plaid skirt in dismay, and then back at her mother. Her eyes filled with tears.

"We—we've been to see Daddy!" she blurted.

Heath gave a groan, and Laurel bit her lip. Goldenrod stared down at her hands.

Mrs. Madder smiled incredulously. "To see your father? But how? You couldn't have gone all the way to Connecticut and back in one afternoon!"

"But we did," Susan said with a sigh. As the others glared at her, she said defiantly, "Well, we *have* to tell her now! What else can we do?"

She turned back to her mother and said in a matter-of-fact voice, "We went to Danbury and saw Daddy's studio, and then there was a thunderstorm, and that's how we got so wet."

Mrs. Madder stared from one to another, rubbing her forehead as if it hurt. They hoped her toothache was better, at least. Then she looked at Val, who never exaggerated or made things up. "Val?" she said.

Slowly Val nodded.

Mrs. Madder leaned back in her chair and closed her eyes. "All right," she said. "I believe you. I guess I have to believe you. Now suppose you tell me all about it."

So they did, beginning with the accidental trip to Gorseville and ending with the house by the railroad tracks in Danbury. They skipped over a few details, like Miss Hepatica's shotgun and Venice sinking into the Grand Canal and Heath's getting stuck on the mountain. But they told her about Wyoming and Laurel winding up in the water trough, which made her laugh; and

about St. Martin and Christophe (but not the barracuda) and how they'd had to leave their clothes behind.

"I'm sorry about your hat, Mother," Laurel said.

"Oh," said Mrs. Madder, a little wildly. "What's one
old hat, more or less?"

But when they came to that afternoon's trip to Danbury, she listened quietly. A mixture of emotions—sadness, amusement, affection—crossed her face as they described their father's reception of them.

"I suppose he's still keeping his work hidden away,"
she said with a sigh, when Laurel mentioned the storeroom. "He'll sell a piece when he gets hard up for
money, but otherwise . . ." She shrugged. "He's quite
well known, you know. People are always trying to get
in to see him."

"Oh!" Daisy clapped a hand to her mouth. "I forgot
to tell him about the money he owes that man on Main
Street."

Mrs. Madder smiled, a little wryly. Then she gave her
youngest child a thoughtful look. "What did you think
of your father, Daisy?"

"Well . . ." Daisy hesitated. "He's very nice, but—he
isn't a very *fatherly* kind of man, is he?"

"No," her mother agreed. Nor a husbandly one,
either, she might have added.

"So," said Daisy, "I decided not to ask him to come
home with us. I don't think it would work out," she explained in her most grown-up voice.

Mrs. Madder hid a smile. "What about the rest of
you?" she said, glancing around the room.

Heath and Susan looked at each other. "We're not
mad at him any more," Heath said.

"I didn't know you ever were," Mrs. Madder said in distress. She shook her head at herself. "I suppose I should have talked to you more," she said. "But some things are hard to explain."

"It was better this way," Laurel told her earnestly. "I mean—well, seeing for ourselves."

Val said, "And maybe we can get to know him better when we're older."

Mrs. Madder nodded, thinking he might be right. Then she asked casually, plucking at a loose thread in her skirt, "Did he say anything about me?"

"Well . . ." Heath frowned, trying to remember. "He talked about my eyes," he said. "How they were just like yours."

"And he has one of your pictures," Laurel added.

Then Goldenrod, who had been sitting silent and tense on the edge of the couch throughout the entire re-cital, spoke up for the first time. "He thinks about you a lot, though," she said and turned her head to look at Mrs. Madder.

No one questioned this statement or wondered how Goldenrod knew. Somehow they realized it was true.

Mrs. Madder sighed and sat back, smiling a little. Then she glanced back at Goldenrod and her expression changed.

"Children," she said briskly, "it's time you got out of those wet clothes. Run along now and change. I want to talk to Goldenrod."

Laurel saw how Goldenrod flinched at this, seeming to shrink into herself. She lingered a moment before she left the room, to make sure Goldenrod didn't start cross-ing her arms and legs. She could feel how much Golden-rod wanted to be anywhere but in this room. But her position didn't change. Reluctantly, Laurel followed the others upstairs.

Mrs. Madder went to sit beside Goldenrod on the couch. She couldn't see the girl's face; it was hidden by the bright curtain of her hair. After a moment she said gently, "I'm not angry with you, Goldenrod."

In a low voice, Goldenrod said, "Maybe you just don't believe any of it."

"Oh, I do."

Mrs. Madder smiled to herself, thinking of the strange paintings upstairs in her studio.

"But what I don't understand is *why*. Oh," she said, as Goldenrod turned her head sharply, "I understand why you've given the children all these trips, and what fun it's been for them, and how much they've learned. I'm grateful to you. Yes," she said, as the green eyes widened, "I am. I only wish I could have gone along on some of them."

She gave a little laugh, remembering the palm trees, the white snow painting, the pigeons and the horses and the bright flowers.

Then she went on seriously, "It's you I'm wondering about, Goldenrod. Why you began taking the trips in the first place. . . . What you were running away from."

For a moment she thought Goldenrod wasn't going to answer. Then she shrugged and said in a muffled voice, "Other people, I guess."

Mrs. Madder nodded. "I thought so. When you were a little girl and something went wrong—maybe when your parents scolded you—that's when you discovered you could go away, wasn't it? Only for a little while, maybe, but still . . . you could get away from all the things that upset you. And if you were careful, nobody would even know you'd been gone. Isn't that how it started?" she asked softly.

Goldenrod shrugged again. "If you knew what my parents were like—" Her voice was bitter. "Fighting all the time, and when they got tired of fighting with each other, they took it out on me. I didn't have any brothers or sisters, I didn't even have a cat—"

Her voice trembled. "So . . . you're right. Sometimes I just had to get away. And then, finally, I just stayed away. For good. There's a way I can do that, but —" She shook her head. "I guess I don't want to tell you about that."

Mrs. Madder put a hand on Goldenrod's shoulder, feeling how tense and jumpy the girl still was. "And this time? What brought you here, Goldenrod? To a town where you didn't know anyone and a job in a supermarket?"

Goldenrod got up suddenly and went over to the fireplace, where she stood with her back to Mrs. Madder, staring up at the willow painting over the mantel.

"I got married," she said at last.

If Mrs. Madder was surprised, she didn't show it. She waited silently.

"He's a wonderful guy," Goldenrod said, in such a dreary voice that Mrs. Madder couldn't help smiling a little. "For a while were very happy. Happier than I'd ever been before."

She swallowed hard. It was a moment before she could go on. "And then—he wanted a baby. He wanted to start a family. But I didn't. I said nothing doing, I knew what families were like. As long as there were just the two of us, everything was okay. But suppose we stopped getting along with each other?" Her voice rose. "Suppose we wanted to split, and we couldn't because of the kids? Like my parents, they were always saying they only stuck it out because of me—"

She stopped and took a deep, shaky breath. "But Tom said it didn't have to be that way. And . . . well, he kept on at me about starting a family, and after a while I couldn't take it any more. So—I left."

Goldenrod put her face in her hands and began to cry.

Mrs. Madder wanted to go to her and comfort her, but something held her back. Maybe it was the old feeling that if you tried to get too close to Goldenrod, she'd slip away somehow. She wondered if Tom had felt that way, too, and hoped that having a baby would hold her to him.

"But he was right!" Goldenrod wailed. "Tom was right! Now that I've seen what a real family can be like— even if there *is* only one parent. . . . But it's too late, he'd never take me back now. And even if he did, how could I ever explain to him?"

"About your trips, you mean?"

"Yes. I never told him, because I never thought I'd want to leave him, not even for a little while. And then, when I did leave—" She was crying again.

This time Mrs. Madder did go to her, putting an arm around the thin shoulders. "You just left, is that it?"

"I was—I was cooking breakfast, and Tom was taking a shower, and all of a sudden I couldn't take it any more. So I sat down at the kitchen table, and—and the eggs must have got all burned!"

Mrs. Madder couldn't help laughing at that, and after a moment Goldenrod managed a watery smile.

"Now listen, Goldenrod," Mrs. Madder said gently.

"For one thing, you're still pretty young to be thinking of having a baby." Goldenrod shook her head violently, but Mrs. Madder persisted. "And a baby can be a lot of work. There'd be times when you'd feel—well, trapped, tied down to the house and the baby. You might be tempted to leave, just for a little while, when things got too much for you."

"I wouldn't! I wouldn't ever want to leave my baby!"

Remembering the diapers and formulas and sleepless nights, Mrs. Madder wasn't so sure; but she went on. "Anyway, I think you'd have to explain about the trips to Tom if you did go back. It would be only fair to him, don't you think?"

After a moment, Goldenrod nodded slowly. "But what if he didn't want me after that?" she whispered. "After he knew?"

"He might not," Mrs. Madder said honestly. "But that's a chance you'd have to take."

Goldenrod stood still, thinking about this. Mrs. Madder found a Kleenex and gave it to her.

"I don't know," Goldenrod said after a while. She blew her nose. "I just don't know." She turned her wide green eyes on Mrs. Madder's. The lashes were wet, but there was no other sign that she'd been crying. "You won't tell *them* about all this, will you?" she said anxiously. "The kids, I mean. They might not understand."

Mrs. Madder thought they probably would—the older ones, anyway—but she said, "Of course not."

"Or—or anyone else? I mean, Tom may have been looking for me—"

"Oh, Goldenrod!" Mrs. Madder gave her a little shake. "Don't you know by now that you can trust me?"

She meant it; but all the same, she couldn't help

154

thinking, rather grimly, about the police, perhaps the Missing Persons Bureau, and feeling a little sorry for Tom.

She said, "I know you need time to think things over. So let's just go on the way we have been—all right? You can stay on with us as long as you like; and then, if you do decide to go back—" Mrs. Madder shrugged. "Well, I guess you can just go, can't you? Is it a G place—where Tom is?"

Goldenrod nodded, smiling a little. "That's how I met him," she said. She looked at Mrs. Madder. "Do you really mean that—about my staying? You don't want me to leave?"

"Of course I don't! I don't know what we'd do without you."

To Mrs. Madder's surprise, Goldenrod gave her a quick, shy hug and then turned away to gaze again at the painting over the mantel. "You know, I'm beginning to see what you mean about that willow tree. . . . I guess you won't want us to take any more trips though, will you?"

As Mrs. Madder hesitated, the children trooped back into the room, dressed in dry clothes now, and trying to contain their curiosity.

Heath had caught the word "trips." He looked from Goldenrod to his mother, decided everything was all right after all, and said eagerly, "Now that you understand about the trips, it's okay, isn't it, Mother? Gosh, there're so many places we still have to get to! It's Val's turn again, I guess, if we're starting over . . . unless maybe Goldenrod wants to go again. We could go to the Gobi Desert or the Grand Canyon or—"

"It seems to me it's *my* turn for a trip," Mrs. Madder

interrupted, to everyone's astonishment.

Goldenrod turned a startled glance on her, and then grinned.

"Well, I'd like to try it at least once," Mrs. Madder said mildly. "Unless I'm too old. Maybe it won't work with a grown-up."

"I think it will," Goldenrod said, still smiling. "It depends on the kind of grown-up."

They exchanged a long look; and for that moment Goldenrod became clear and solid at last for Mrs. Madder—a person with definite outlines, with a past, a present, and (Mrs. Madder hoped) a future as well.

The children were clamoring with excitement, pouring out ideas for *R* places. A whole new initial to work with!

"Let's go to the Rhine!" said Susan, who had been studying Germany in school. "That's a river, and there are all these darling castles that look just like toys—"

"The Rio Grande," Val interrupted. "That's a *real* river."

"Let's go to Russia!" said Heath.

"What about Rome?" said Laurel. "Oh, Mother, you'd love to go to Rome, wouldn't you? All the paintings and statues and—"

"Just let me think a minute," Mrs. Madder said.

She began to pace around the room, a faraway look in her eyes. They waited suspensefully . . . but when she spoke, it wasn't of mountains or rivers or famous cities.

"Rhode Island," she said. "There's a place in Rhode Island I've always wanted to go back to."

"Oh, Mother!" they groaned.

Daisy said in disdain, "But Rhode Island's so *little!*"

Just a speck on the map in her classroom, she meant.

"Gosh," Heath said disgustedly. "Think of all the neat places there are in the world to choose from—and she has to choose Rhode Island!"

"Never mind," said Goldenrod in a stern voice that made them all look at her guiltily. "You kids know the rules. And if Rhode Island's where your mother wants to go, that's where we're going."

"Not for a while, though," Mrs. Madder said. "Not until the weather gets a little warmer. It's a beach I want to go to," she explained. "And anyhow, there's a painting I'll probably have to finish first."

Of Danbury, she was thinking resignedly. She hoped it wouldn't have to be a picture of Main Street. But it wasn't. As the painting began to take shape in her mind, to grow and fill the corners of the canvas, it was just a picture of a room—a big, bare room lighted by tall windows, with the solitary figure of a man leaning against a dusty workbench.

Chapter 13 *Mrs. Madder's Trip*

"It doesn't matter if it's not exactly the same beach," Mrs. Madder said to Goldenrod on the Sunday morning of their trip to Rhode Island. "Just so it's the same *kind* of beach—long and narrow, with a lighthouse at the end. The ocean's one one side, and the bay's on the other."

When Goldenrod looked puzzled, she explained, "It's really a spit of land, like a finger pointing out to sea. And there should be swans in the bay, if possible."

"Swans," Goldenrod repeated uneasily. "Maybe I'd better look at a picture of a swan first. I mean, I know they're white and they have long necks—"

"You might wind up with a plain old seagull," Susan told her mother.

"Or a pelican," Val said, with a grin.

"Oh, well, the swans aren't really important," Mrs.

Madder said. "Just as long as the stones are there—those beautiful pale colors . . ."

Her voice trailed off. She was remembering a long-ago walk with her husband along a Rhode Island beach. They had held hands and talked; but all the while, Mrs. Madder was seeing colors, contrasts, outlines, the subtle play of light and shadow—while he, no doubt, was studying the shapes of waves and rocks with his sculptor's eyes. Mrs. Madder smiled to herself, a little sadly.

She looked at her watch and said, "Well, let's get going, shall we? I want to begin on the painting the minute we get back, and I'll need all the daylight I can get."

"The painting?" Laurel said.

Val groaned. "Is *that* what this is all about?"

"Of course," their mother said in surprise. "What else? I tried to paint that beach all those years ago, but I didn't really have the technique then to get it right." Her eyes narrowed. She hoped the light would be right for the effect she wanted. If not—

"Mother!" Susan was looking at her reproachfully. "We can't go at all unless you start concentrating."

"Oh, yes." Mrs. Madder gave herself a mental shake. "Now—tell me again just what it is I have to do."

They did, and after a final check, they were ready to leave. Sweaters and windbreakers, because in early April it would still be cold at the beach; a picnic basket packed with sandwiches and hard-boiled eggs and a thermos of hot cocoa; the field glasses, in case there were any interesting birds or ships or people to be seen. . . .

"You mean you haven't been taking the field glasses with you all along?" Mrs. Madder demanded. "Why, think of all the things you must have missed! You see, you really do need me along to arrange things properly."

The children grinned at each other and hoped their mother wasn't going to be disappointed. After all, a grown-up . . . maybe it wouldn't work, no matter what Goldenrod said. If it didn't—well, Laurel thought, it was a nice day here at home. They could always take the car and have a picnic out in the country somewhere.

It took longer this time—a good five minutes of sitting very still in the living room and trying not to fidget—but it did work. Or at least, as Susan pointed out afterwards, they wound up on a beach like the one their mother had described. As for its being in Rhode Island—well, with only a lighthouse and a swan to go by, how could anyone tell?

"Oh, what a strange feeling!" Mrs. Madder exclaimed, when she opened her eyes at last. "As if your bones were dissolving. . . ."

Then she sniffed the cold salt breeze; she blinked and looked around her with astonishment. "Why it is!" she said. "It looks like the very same beach!"

"But it's all foggy here," Daisy complained, shivering.

"Oh, that's just mist," her mother declared confidently. "It'll burn off soon."

Even as she spoke, the white haze around them brightened. In the pearly light, the tumbled waves of the ocean shone steel-blue, with racing whitecaps. The calmer waters of the bay to their right gleamed a softer blue, the surface only wrinkled by the strong wind blowing in off the sea.

"Perfect!" Mrs. Madder exclaimed, looking down the long sandy point to the lighthouse, dimly visible at its tip. "The light's even better than it was the other time. What a wonderful way to travel!" she said, turning enthusiastically to Goldenrod. "No maps to bother with, no gas to buy, no time for the children to get bored and start fighting in the back seat. . . . And oh, just smell that air!"

Goldenrod smiled, but she looked a little doubtful. It really was quite cold, standing there in the wind. The children were gazing about them in some dismay.

"But what are we going to *do?*" Val asked, for all of them.

"Why, we're going to walk, of course," said Mrs. Madder. "What else?" And she set off briskly along the beach.

Val and Heath looked at each other, shrugged, and picked up the heavy picnic basket between them.

"Are we going all the way out to the lighthouse?" Susan said anxiously, hurrying to catch up with her mother.

"Heavens, no! That's a lot farther than it looks—several miles, probably. No, I thought we'd just wander along until we find a good place for our picnic, and then come back."

It didn't sound like much of a program to Susan, but she plodded along dutifully. They were keeping to the center of the point, which was high and rounded like the crown of a road. The sand was a soft pale gray here, edged on the bay side by silvery green beach grasses. At first Susan couldn't see what her mother meant about the colors. Surely all the color was in the water, not here on this pale, same-colored beach.

Then she began to look more attentively at the hundreds of small stones underfoot. They were smooth and rounded, bleached by the sun and salt air to the most subtle and delicate shades: rose, amber, sage green, mauve, blue, coral, dove gray. . . . As Mrs. Madder

161

said, the more you looked, the more you seemed to see.

"I thought maybe you'd bring a sketchbook or something with you," Goldenrod said shyly, as Mrs. Madder paused to study the zigzag line of a slatted snow fence against a dune.

"I never do," she replied absently. "I've got to have the whole thing in my head anyhow, and sketches just seem to get in the way. . . . I suppose we could take some stones back with us, though. Susan, why don't you fill your pockets, and we can sort them out later."

Susan looked questioningly at Goldenrod, who shook her head. "We can't, Mother," she said. "We can't take anything back, remember?"

"Oh, well—they'd look different at home, anyway. It's the light." Mrs. Madder glanced up. The haze was only a gauzy film now over a pale blue sky. "Oh, dear," she said. "I hope it's not going to get *too* sunny."

Just then Laurel gave a shout. She had the field glasses and had been keeping to the bay side of the point, stopping from time to time to scan the water for birds. She'd seen plenty of gulls and terns; but now at last she'd spotted a swan.

The others crowded around her, begging for a chance at the glasses. "You don't need them now, anyway," she said. "He's swimming this way."

They had seen swans before, of course, in city parks—aloof and haughty, except when they were making a greedy dash for the crumbs tossed out by their human admirers. But a swan alone in the wild seemed a different creature altogether: strange and majestic, gliding slowly over the icy blue waters of the bay, miles from cities and crowds. As they watched, it dipped its orange beak several times, as if testing the water, and then dived. It was gone so long beneath the surface that Daisy began to worry about it.

"Maybe it forgot to take a deep enough breath," she said anxiously.

But the swan reappeared, gliding calmly onward as if refreshed by its cold bath. Or maybe it didn't even feel the cold. They could see how its thick white feathers protected it, shedding the water and cushioning it from the bitter wind.

"A mute swan," Mrs. Madder said, her own voice hushed. "It makes no noise. But they say it sings just before it dies."

Goldenrod shivered, though the sun was much warmer now. "It's beautiful," she said. "But it looks so alone."

"It probably has a mate nearby," Heath assured her; but Goldenrod didn't look convinced. Mrs. Madder gave her a thoughtful glance before she turned away.

"See those big dunes up ahead?" she said, pointing. "That looks like a good place to have lunch, where we can get out of the wind."

Val groaned. "All that way?" He hefted the picnic basket. "This thing's heavy, you know."

"I'll carry it for a while," his mother said. "Why don't you all go down along the beach? The walking's easier there. I'll meet you at the dunes."

The children didn't need any urging. With a whoop, they raced across the point to the ocean side, where the sand was hard and flat. Goldenrod hesitated, offering to take the picnic basket; but Mrs. Madder said she didn't mind, and anyway, she'd just as soon be by herself for a while—"just moseying along," as she put it.

"Try to keep the children out of the water, won't

you?" she added, as Goldenrod set off after them. "It would be nice if they could come home dry for once."

But it was already too late for that, as Goldenrod found when she arrived on the beach. Susan and Daisy were playing Can't Catch Me with the waves, and Daisy had already been caught, judging by the soaked cuffs of her jeans. A little further on, Val and Laurel were skipping stones out into the choppy surf and arguing about how many times their stones had jumped.

"Six!" Laurel insisted.

"It was not," Val scoffed. "Four at the most."

They turned to Goldenrod as she came toward them.

"You count, Goldenrod," Laurel said. "That way it'll be fair."

A large wave was cresting behind them. "Look out!" said Goldenrod, as the wave broke with a muffled explosion and came rushing up onto the beach in a flurry of green and white.

They leaped away, but not in time. The foam swirled up around their sneakers and socks before sinking away into the sand with a hiss of tiny bubbles.

"Wow! Is that cold!" Laurel looked down ruefully at her wet feet. "Not like the water in St. Martin. . . ." She sighed. "I wonder if there's an island down there beginning with *L*. Or maybe Susan could choose another *S* one when her turn comes again."

"It's my turn next, though," Val reminded her.

Goldenrod looked at them. She seemed about to say something—but then just smiled and shook her head. They were always to remember the way she looked just then, with the wind whipping back the golden froth of her hair, her eyes as green and changeable as the sea itself.

Then she turned abruptly and glanced along the beach. "Where's Heath?" she asked.

They shrugged. "He walked on up the beach by himself," Laurel said. "You know Heath."

But Goldenrod frowned. "It looks like the fog is coming in again. Look—you can hardly see the lighthouse any more."

They strained their eyes. She was right: the lighthouse was only a vague white blur now in the thick gray cloud that had gathered about the tip of the point. This wasn't the fine sea mist that had greeted them on their arrival; this was a real fog, they realized, rolling silently in from the sea, erasing landmarks, smothering all light and color in its path.

"Daisy! Susan!" Goldenrod called. "We'd better get going."

As they came running up, Susan said, "Look what I found! Here, Goldenrod, it's for you." She handed Goldenrod a large, shiny pink shell with a fluted rim. "It's the kind you can hear the ocean in, I think. It's hard to tell," she explained, "with the ocean making so much noise already. But maybe when you get it home . . ."

"Thank you, Susan. It's beautiful." Goldenrod stroked the satiny contours of the shell, smiling with pleasure. Then she glanced up the beach again. There was still no sign of Heath.

"Maybe he's already gone up to the dunes," Val suggested.

"Well, we can't lose him, anyway," Laurel said. She pointed to the line of Heath's footprints leading away up the beach.

They started off, wet sneakers squelching in the damp sand. For a while Daisy scampered ahead, dodging around in circles and figure eights, making patterns in the sand. But she soon tired of that and rejoined the others. Although the wind had dropped, the air was damp and chilly now, the sun only a pale metallic gleam on the surface of the ocean as the fog advanced.

Once they caught a glimpse of Mrs. Madder making her way steadily along the top of the spit. They called, and she waved back. But when they yelled "Fog!" and pointed, she cupped her ears and shrugged to show she couldn't hear; then gestured toward the dunes ahead and moved on.

Goldenrod said, "Why don't you all go up with your mother? I'll find Heath."

"But he can't have gone much further," Susan pointed out. "Look how narrow the beach is getting."

It was true: there was a great jumble of rocks just ahead, where the point began to curve slightly out to sea. The broad stretch of sand on which they'd been walking had begun to dwindle to a narrow strip, made even narrower by the incoming tide. Still Heath's footprints led steadily onward.

"I hope he didn't decide to go rock climbing in the fog," Val said. "He never does pay any attention to the weather."

Daisy said, "Well, at least there's no mountain to fall off of here."

But Laurel, squinting ahead into the swirling mist, thought a fall here might be almost as bad. She could hear the boom of the waves against the rocky tip of the point, and thought with a shiver of what one careless step might mean.

"Hey!" Susan, who was in the lead, stopped short.

"This is where the beach ends, I guess. But which way did he go?"

They saw what she meant. The rocks crowded in around a last small triangle of sand; but there was no way to tell if Heath had crossed it. The sea was already washing in and out, and any footprints had gone forever.

They stood uncertainly, looking at the rocks ahead of them, sharp and slimy with weed and spray and the fog-laden air.

"He wouldn't have gone that way," Laurel said, with more assurance than she felt. "Even Heath has more sense."

Val said, "But the fog probably wasn't as bad when he got here."

"Well," Goldenrod said firmly, "whether he did or not, we're not going up there after him. Let's head back for the dunes. Heath's probably there by now, anyway."

A wave crashed against the rocks nearby, drenching them with cold salt spray. Soon the area where they stood would be under water. Without further argument, they followed Goldenrod back along the beach to a point where they could scramble up onto higher ground.

"Gosh," said Susan, as they arrived at the top. "How are we ever going to tell which dune?"

The fog was thicker here and growing denser by the moment. Until now, they'd at least had the contrast of beach and sea to guide them. Here there was only low scrub growth, and a confused impression of the billowing shapes of dunes ahead of them. Seagulls mewed somewhere overhead; and now they heard the unmistakable deep voice of a foghorn out to sea. Or was it coming from the lighthouse itself? Already the fog was confusing their sense of direction.

"We'd better start calling," Goldenrod said and put a hand on Daisy's arm. "No, don't move, Daisy. If we start wandering around, we'll get lost for sure. Your mother's bound to hear us if we yell loud enough. And Heath, too."

"Some picnic this is going to be," Val grumbled. "If we ever catch up with it."

They called and yelled until they were hoarse. Only the gulls and the foghorn answered them.

Val stopped thinking about his stomach then and tried to visualize the direction in which his mother had been heading the last time they saw her.

"I think if we went straight ahead a little way, and then bore over to the right. . . ." He hesitated. "We'd better hold hands, though."

This was an all-too-grim reminder of their experience on the mountain ledge. And now it wasn't only Heath who was in trouble—their mother might be, too. But nobody said anything; there seemed nothing else to do.

Slowly, strung out in a line with Val (again) in the lead, they felt their way along through the white murk. Briars tore at their pants legs, the thorns of beach roses scratched their hands and arms. From time to time they stopped to yell and listen.

And then, just as they were deciding they'd gone too far to the right, they heard a faint answering cry.

They yelled. The cry came again.

"Well, at least we know where Mother is," Laurel said in relief. "If she'll just keep calling . . ."

She did, but it didn't turn out to be that simple. The fog not only played tricks with distance and direction, it distorted sound as well. Sometimes the call seemed to come from straight ahead of them; at other times from slightly to their left or right.

They blundered along more and more slowly, straining their ears to listen, correcting their direction so many times that they began to worry about going around in circles. The fog was a thick white wall now that pressed against them at every turn.

Suddenly Val said *"Oof!"* and stumbled over something, bringing Susan down with him.

Heath's voice said irritably, "Hey—watch it!"

"Heath!" Daisy peered down at the ground. "What are you doing? Did you hurt yourself?"

Heath was on all fours in the sand. He said, "I'm following Mother's footprints. Come on, you can see a lot better down here. I don't think it's much farther."

"Why didn't you let us know where you were?" Laurel demanded, as they all got down on their hands and knees and began to crawl along after Heath.

"I figured it would just confuse you if I started yelling, too. Val, get off my ankle, will you?"

It was true that at ground level there was some visibility—not much, but enough for Heath to follow the footprints that wound in and out of clumps of beach grass and small dunes. He explained that he'd gone up on the rocks ("just to see what I could see"), but had turned back as the fog closed in, in time to catch a distant glimpse of his mother making for a high pile of dunes on the bay side. By the time he got back down onto the sand, he could no longer see the dunes—or much of anything—but he had a pretty good idea of the direction she'd taken. So he began looking for her footprints.

"Let's just hope they're Mother's and not somebody else's," Laurel said, pulling a pricker out of the palm of her hand.

"Whose else could they be?" Susan demanded. (She certainly wasn't going to worry about the Abominable Snowman here at sea level.)

Goldenrod, who was crawling along at the end of the line, began to laugh suddenly. It was a fresh, open kind of laugh—the kind they rarely heard from her.

"You kids!" she said. "Blizzards and floods and thunderstorms—and now fog. About the only thing we haven't had is a hurricane. Oh, well—just think of all the stories I can tell my grandchildren someday."

Daisy said practically, "But you haven't even got a child yet, Goldenrod. You have to have children before you can have grandchildren."

"I know," Goldenrod said, her voice sobering.

Heath was leading them up the slippery side of a high dune. "Mother," he called.

"I'm right here," said Mrs. Madder, so close that they all jumped.

Heath reached the top and peered down at his mother. She was sitting in a pocket of soft sand, her back resting comfortably against a dune, with the picnic basket beside her. The fog hadn't settled here, for some reason, though it made a thick white roof overhead.

"I was getting awfully hungry," Mrs. Madder said, as they scrambled down beside her. "But I decided I'd better wait for you."

"Weren't you even *worried?*" Susan said indignantly.

"Oh, you had Goldenrod with you," Mrs. Madder said carelessly. "And Heath has a good sense of direction."

170

They decided not to explain that they'd almost lost Heath.

"Anyway, it was so peaceful here, I almost fell asleep."

She was handing out sandwiches and hard-boiled eggs; Laurel noticed that her hands trembled a little. She hadn't been quite so unconcerned as she made out. "The only thing is, I hope the fog lifts pretty soon, because we'll have a hard time finding our way back otherwise."

Heath smiled, and Daisy began to giggle.

"Oh, that's right," Mrs. Madder said in a relieved tone. "I forgot—we can just *go*, can't we, whenever we're ready? This really is a marvelous way to travel!" She smiled at Goldenrod.

But Goldenrod was looking down at the pink shell, which she'd somehow managed to hold onto during their ramblings in the fog. She sat turning it over and over in her hands, her expression hidden from them. She didn't seem very hungry, either, they noticed. She drank some hot cocoa, but refused a sandwich.

The cocoa warmed them momentarily, but by the time they'd finished eating, they realized how cold and damp they were. The fog showed no signs of lifting; it still hung above them in a solid mass.

"Well," Mrs. Madder said with a sigh, putting the last scrap of waxed paper back in the picnic basket, "I suppose it's time we left. There's certainly nothing more to see, and I want to begin work on the painting while everything's still fresh in my mind."

Goldenrod said in a low voice, "I hope it turns out the way you want it to. The colors, and all."

Mrs. Madder was settling herself into a cross-legged position on the sand. "Well," she said, "you can judge for yourself, as soon as it's finished."

Val saw the tiny shake of Goldenrod's head; and at the same moment, Laurel realized that Goldenrod was still holding the shell. She had crossed her arms, but the shell remained firmly grasped in one hand.

"Goldenrod!" Laurel said in alarm. "The shell—you can't take it back with you! Remember?"

"That's right," said Susan. "I forgot, when I gave it to you."

"Why can't she take it back?" Daisy asked.

"Because—" Laurel stopped, realizing she didn't know just why. A rule, Goldenrod had said.

Mrs. Madder said impatiently, "Are we going or aren't we? I'm getting stiff in this position." She closed her eyes.

But Goldenrod wasn't quite ready, it seemed. She was looking at the children intently, her eyes moving from face to face. They were reminded uneasily of the moment with their father in the studio doorway. For an instant the green eyes seemed to be glistening with tears. And still she held the shell.

And then they understood.

"You aren't coming back with us, are you?" Laurel said slowly.

"No," Goldenrod told them in a gentle voice. "There's someplace else I have to go now. Your mother can explain about it later. But don't worry—I'll see that you get home all right."

Mrs. Madder opened her eyes then and looked at Goldenrod. After a moment she gave a little nod. "If you're sure," she said.

Goldenrod smiled. "I'm sure," she said, and closed her eyes.

"Goldenrod!" said Heath.

"Oh, please don't go away," Daisy pleaded.

"No!" Susan cried. "Don't leave us! Goldenrod—you *can't* leave us!"

But Goldenrod's face had gone still and pale with concentration. Already the children's eyelids were drooping, and their limbs felt heavy and soft, drowsy with sleep. The drift was beginning.

Laurel knew better than to try to fight it. And perhaps Val did, too.

"We'll miss you, Goldenrod," he said into the stillness.

And then the fog closed in and over them.

Chapter 14 Pearly

When the doorbell rang one bright Saturday morning in June, Mrs. Madder was sitting at the corner desk in the living room, writing a letter. It was the kind of letter she particularly disliked writing—full of appeals and explanations and apologies. What made it worse was the fact that the letter was addressed to Miss Vetch.

But after nearly two months of baby-sitters who didn't show up (their car wouldn't start) or who had to leave early (they had to wash their hair) or who couldn't be bothered to learn the children's names (too many of them), Mrs. Madder was resigned. She would simply have to hire a housekeeper again. And however one felt about Miss Vetch, she was certainly reliable, and a good cook, and the kind of person who always remembered to write down telephone messages. . . .

"Children?" Mrs. Madder called, as the doorbell rang a second time. But no one seemed to be within earshot. With a sigh, she got and went to answer it.

"Mrs. Madder?"

A young black woman stood on the doorstep, smiling up at Mrs. Madder so infectiously that Mrs. Madder immediately smiled back. Her face was round and dimpled, and the smile displayed a row of small, perfect white teeth. She wore a long, flowing, purple dress with silver embroidery, and looked rather as Mrs. Madder imagined a royal African princess might look—serene, good-humored, and self-possessed.

"I understand you've been looking for a baby-sitter," said this exotic caller, in a light, pleasant voice that had a trace of Southern accent.

"Well, yes. I mean, I certainly have!" said Mrs. Madder. "But how—?"

She broke off, staring at the car drawn up beside the curb. It was an old black Volkswagen, its dull paintwork dappled with sunlight under the fluttering new leaves of the trees.

Her visitor followed the glance. "Goldenrod said I might as well use it," she said calmly, "as long as I was coming to live around here."

"Goldenrod—?"

"I guess the way things were, she didn't exactly have time to collect it before she left. Being in something of a hurry, you might say."

"Yes," Mrs. Madder agreed, rather faintly. "I mean, no. But who—"

"Anyhow, Goldenrod said maybe you could use a hand with the kids," the young woman went on in a businesslike way. "If you haven't already found someone, that is. I'll be teaching school here in the fall—second grade. But I'd have my afternoons free."

"The fall. . . ." Mrs. Madder forgot her curiosity about Goldenrod long enough to feel disappointed; she'd already taken a liking to this rather surprising young woman. "The only trouble is, I really need someone now. What with school letting out—and I don't have my vacation until August." She shook her head.

"I'm also looking for a place to live," her visitor explained. "If you had a room to spare . . ." She shrugged. "Well, I thought maybe we might come to some arrangement. I'll be taking some courses in the city this summer, but they're all in the evenings. So I'd be around during the day to keep an eye on things. I don't want to do housework," she added firmly. "But I understand the kids take care of all that."

"Oh—yes. Yes, they do."

Mrs. Madder was thinking rapidly. A room. . . . Of course they had a room! Miss Vetch's old room at the back of the house, full now of discarded clothing and broken lamps and old toys. . . . No one had wanted to live in it. They said it smelled of Miss Vetch; which was ridiculous, all traces of Miss Vetch's lily-of-the-valley perfume having long since vanished.

Anyway, it was a nice big room, and if the things could be cleared out somehow—maybe they could have a tag sale—this young woman would probably find it quite pleasant, not having known Miss Vetch.

"I do like to cook, though," her visitor was saying. "That is, if you don't mind other people messing around in your kitchen."

She gave Mrs. Madder that delightful dimpled smile again. It was an *inside* kind of smile, as Val would say—

not just something that happened to the outside of her face.

"Not at all," Mrs. Madder said, smiling back. "I don't have much time to cook myself, anyway, so. . . ."

Her voice trailed off distractedly; she simply *had* to ask.

"How is Goldenrod?" she said. "We haven't heard anything from her."

"I know." The young woman sighed. "She never was much for letter writing. But she's fine. She and Tom—they're both fine. She wanted me to be sure and tell you that. And she's got a new job, working for a travel agency."

"A travel agency," Mrs. Madder repeated in some alarm. Good heavens! Goldenrod was a whole travel agency in herself, if only people knew. I just hope she's staying put, she thought.

"I'm sure she's very good at it," she said, rather lamely. "I mean, with her experience—" She broke off to stare hard at her visitor. "Do *you* do any . . . traveling?"

"Me?" She threw back her head and laughed—a good, rich, chuckly kind of laugh. "No, ma'am. The only traveling I plan to do is around town in that old car of Goldenrod's, and I don't suppose that'll take me very far."

Mrs. Madder sighed. "Well, I have to admit that's something of a relief. Not that it wasn't interesting while it lasted, of course."

They smiled at each other with understanding, and with something more—affection for Goldenrod, and concern for her. Mrs. Madder thought of the unfinished portrait in her studio. The shape of the face was right, and

177

the hair; but the eyes . . . the eyes flickered and changed and refused to stay still beneath her brush. Maybe the portrait should just be left that way: unfinished.

Mrs. Madder realized suddenly that she'd kept her visitor standing on the doorstep all this time. She apologized, saying, "Won't you come in? I do have an extra room, although it's kind of a mess at the moment—"

"I'd rather meet the kids first, if you don't mind," the young woman said, and looked around. "Are they at home?"

"I think they must be around back somewhere," Mrs. Madder said. She led the way across the grass to the path at the side of the house, where they almost collided with Heath.

"Mother," he said breathlessly, "where's the hose?"

"The hose? Why? Is something on fire?"

"No, of course not." Heath scowled. "We've been working in the vegetable garden, and—"

"And Heath hasn't done any weeding at all," Susan announced, marching up with a hoe over her shoulder. "So we said he'd have to do the watering at least, before he takes off on his bike for the whole rest of the day." She glared at Heath. "And if we can't find the sprinkler —well, he'll just have to stand there with the hose for as long as it takes."

"Maybe it'll rain," Heath said hopefully, looking up at the cloudless sky.

There was a commotion from inside Mrs. Teasel's hedge. Then Laurel backed out of it on her hands and knees and stood up. "I found it!" she said triumphantly, holding up a battered sprinkler. Her face was flushed, and bits of leaves and twigs were caught in her long hair. "It must have been there all winter."

"Children!" Mrs. Madder spoke sharply, feeling that her family wasn't showing itself at its best. "We have a guest. Will you all please calm down for a minute?"

But their visitor seemed unperturbed. "Heath, Susan, Laurel . . ." She was naming off the children with an air of pleased recognition. "And here's Val," she added, as Val appeared around the side of the house, carrying a bat and his catcher's mitt.

"Val," Mrs. Madder said, "all of you—I want you to meet a friend of Goldenrod's. She's going to be our new baby-sitter, I hope, and—" She looked around distractedly. "Oh, where's Daisy? Daisy!" she called, and went off to the back yard in search of her.

"Maybe you'll let me borrow your mitt sometime," the young woman said to Val. "I used to be pretty good."

They all stared. Baseball, in that outfit? And a friend of Goldenrod's . . . ? But Goldenrod didn't have any friends, not that they knew of.

She smiled. "You don't think Goldenrod pitched that no-hitter without a good catcher, do you? I don't mean to take anything away from Goldenrod, but I was the brains of that outfit, believe me."

Val frowned thoughtfully. He *had* wondered about that, as a matter of fact. Goldenrod was fast, all right; but when it came to things like learning the hitters' weaknesses, working out strategy—

"Girls' softball league," Heath was saying slowly, in a reminiscent voice. "Back in Ohio. Nineteen and three."

Their visitor nodded, showing her dimples. They found themselves smiling back at her, a little dazedly.

179

Just then Mrs. Madder came back with Daisy in tow. Daisy's face was grimy and tear-stained. "I didn't mean to step on it," she was saying sadly. "And now it won't be able to grow up and have any little tomatoes."

Laurel said, "Oh, Daisy! We've got more tomato plants than we need, anyway. And anyway, never mind about that now. Look—we've got a new baby-sitter, and she's a friend of Goldenrod's!"

Daisy stopped short, gazing open-mouthed at the smiling young black woman in the beautiful purple dress.

"Well," said Mrs. Madder, drawing a deep breath. "Now that we're all here, I want you to meet Goldenrod's friend—"

She stopped, realizing that she'd never even asked the new baby-sitter's name.

"We almost met once before," the young woman said, teasing them a little, her dark eyes brimming with laughter. "You had a long hot walk, and you went swimming in the old swimming hole, and you met Miss Hepatica—"

"Pearly!" the children shouted.

They crowded around her excitedly.

"It's Pearly at last!" said Susan.

Daisy shook her head. "It's Pearly *Everlasting*," she corrected; and her face lit up.

Pearly smiled and took Daisy's hand. "Well, I don't know about that," she said. "But I'll be around for a while, anyway."